ANNIE AND THE BIRDS OF GRACELAND

ISBN: 978-0-9559762-0-9

Acknowledgements

Before you read this novel I thought I'd give special thanks to my family and my friends in particular Mum and Dad for always believing in me allowing me to make my own choices be them right or wrong, freedom is a powerful asset to growing up so thank you.

Jane Dunst thanks for believing only I could write such a tale, big thanks to Yume no Chikara in particular the Director Tammy Keys for her guidance, belief, support and friendship.

Huge thanks to a very talented young man named Daniel Evans who produced the front cover it's like he knew what I wanted and pulled it out of my mind you're a hero and I wish this only to be the beginning for you, good things are bound to follow trust.

To the boys and girls you know who you are three words for you "poetry in motion."

If I've missed out anyone I apologise and in the next book I'll give you some love.

Big thanks to one and all enjoy the novel it's only the beginning.

Peace and Love
D.J.Skerritt

Chapter 1-Born in the stable

Alan Granger ran towards the stable. A mournful scream rang through the night. Alan ran to the source in the dark clutching a torch in his hand, he stopped a moment realising he was being followed.

"Help," shouted an unknown woman from the Granger stable. "Help! Help!"

Alan spun round and saw his son Peter running towards him.

"Dad, I heard a scream from our stable!"

The two men hurled themselves towards the stable and pushed open the door to find a young woman laying on the hay near Russell the horse. She was screaming and rubbing her enormous stomach with a nervous hand. She was pregnant and in distress as her waters had obviously broken.

"Peter," cried the woman, "Peter please help me."

Alan stared at his son who was rooted to the spot; Alan still quite confused went without a word towards the young woman who was already starting to push.

Alan leaned towards her and lifted her head; he then placed her head on the hay.

She pushed with all her might, leaving Alan only seconds to bend backwards and grab the head and the body of the baby.

"It's a girl! It's a little girl," exclaimed Peter who had approached them gingerly.

Two women now entered the stable and Alan recognised the voices of Carla his wife and his daughter-in-law Kirsty who was shouting behind him.

"What happened?" concerned Carla who understood nothing.

She went towards Alan and they both helped the woman, Alan gave the little baby to his son, while he bent more closely towards the woman's face. Her eyes were already dimming, the woman tried to say something to Alan, but no sound left her mouth. The old man tried to support her head to help her speak, however it was in vain as she gently closed her eyes and passed on.

As Alan sat in his wheelchair he could not believe his eyes, it had been eight years since that day, almost nine years since the birth of Annie and he remembered it as if it was yesterday. The little baby girl whom was born in the stable was the size of a small tree, she had long jet-black hair, which covered half of her body and she was so beautiful. She resembled her mother so much that every time Alan looked at Annie, he could see the woman who had given her life, he also saw his son give back the baby to his mother Carla as Kirsty started stirring up the neighbours.

Carla had called the ambulance and a male nurse had taken the time of death of the woman. She was a stranger to them, yet Alan remembered that she called his son by his first name.

The police had come and made enquires to find nothing amiss. The woman's body was taken along to the mortuary, at which point Carla decided to raise the orphan. Peter signed the necessary papers under the threat of his mother, as well as Alan asking difficult questions about his relationship with the mystery woman.

Kirsty was so angry and had never forgiven Peter for adopting Annie, especially when he already had twin girls Madge and Madeline with her. Peter did everything in his power to cover up his adultery, pretending to his wife that he did not know the woman who died in their stable. Under the pressure of Kirsty, Peter wanted to take the child to the orphanage, however his mother Carla had threatened to disinherit him and with that statement, he dropped all acts to prevent this. Peter chose to live with Annie as if she were an orphan he had taken in, and not once did he treat her like a daughter.

"Annie, you didn't finish the washing up and you didn't clean the twin's bedroom," bellowed Kirsty as she came down the stairs.

She pulled Annie's ears; the poor little girl cried in pain, her stepmother then dragged her to the kitchen and threw her against the door, in spite of the little girls' cries. Kirsty was so angry; she then pushed her on the floor near the wheelchair of her grandfather. Alan tried to help Annie only to receive a slap at the back of the head.

"Try to help her and you'll see what happens old man!" scolded Kirsty as she pushed the wheelchair out of her way.

Alan's wheelchair knocked against the large sofa, sending the old man to the floor causing him to yelp like a dog, Alan moved towards the crying Annie by crawling, he then took her in his arms to shield her from the bullying. Life had become like this since the death of his wife Carla.

Alan soothed his grandaughter in his arms. He spotted Kirsty coming towards them she dragged Annie out of the arms of the old man and continued her punishment by slapping Annie twice on her bottom; Kirsty struck so hard Annie ceased to wriggle free.

"Annie, Annie!" cried Alan as he crawled towards her in the kitchen, but Kirsty had cut him off, she howled like a banshee.

"Old Fool, you believe that you can always save this orphan, she only gets what she deserves and you will too," said his daughter in-law smugly. She slapped him on the head again and then continued to bully Annie after she rubbed her hands on her robe.

"You Child! That was for disobeying my orders!"

With pride on her face, Kirsty went upstairs to find her daughters who were shouting from the top of the stairs.

"Mum! Mum! This time, you didn't punish Annie well enough. She didn't wash my dress," complained Madge.

"Mum, my pyjamas are still dirty. How will I sleep now?" grilled Madeline

Kirsty was trying to calm them down when the door swung open.

"Dad! Dad!" Screamed the twins, they ran towards their father to tell him what had happened.

"Oh! My sweet daughters, how was the day for my little Princesses?" asked Peter.

He took them in his arms and kissed them both on their cheeks. He heard tears coming from the kitchen he stopped and sighed deeply.

"What has Annie done wrong today?"

"She has been punished by mum, she didn't do her work." answered Madge.

"She refused to do the washing up and spent all the day playing with my doll," added Madeline.

Peter put down his daughters and went towards the kitchen. He found his father carrying Annie on his knees. He looked at the scene with rage. Alan lowered his eyes away from his son, like always.

"You tried to help her again didn't you! How often do I have to tell you that Annie is only a clumsy and stubborn little girl? If she does not listen to my wife, I will send her to the orphanage." growled Peter.

He hadn't finished his sentence when Kirsty butted in by gesturing.

"I didn't even have the time to punish her properly as she ran for safety in your father's arms. She banged against his wheelchair and scratched herself."

Peter once more, blamed his father. Alan kept his eyes fixed on the ground to avoid the judgemental gaze.

He did not have the courage to raise them, as he did not understand the behaviour of his son. He closed his eyelids firmly, not wanting to see or hear what his son would say this time.

"How many times do I have to tell you not to stay in the house, old man? You make Annie stubborn and she no longer manages to do the housework because she must take care of you. I'll have to send you to the care home and you will die there. That is what you deserve!" shouted Peter as he struck the kitchen door.

He took Annie out of the arms of his father and went to lay her down in her room, a small dark corner under the staircase. He put Annie on her mattress and left without as much as a look for her small body.

Later on that night with his heart tight and the tears in his eyes, Alan left the house without a sound. He made the effort to close the door well behind him. He calmly turned the wheels of his wheelchair making sure not to wake the sleepy house as he went into the night.

The old man crossed the empty streets to the small forest covering Ardwick Green Park and Cakebread Street. Alan rolled as quickly as he could towards the exit of the park. He looked on his left and on his right, he saw two owls perched on a tree and heard the owlet scream of another.

Alan nervously pressed his hands on the two wheels of his wheelchair and continued. The old man had almost made it half way when he saw a light coming from a house.

Alan breathed heavily, as he looked at his destination in the distance. He sped up and arrived, he went to knock on the door of the house. An old woman opened and she said to him.

"Come in, I was waiting for you."

"Ah, you were waiting for me!" said Alan while looking at the old woman without expression.

"Well yes! Don't forget that I am a witch who sees all and hears all. You need my help for your grandaughter, Kirsty makes her life very difficult, you want me to tell my daughter not to ill-treat Annie anymore, Alan, you came to me to help you." said the witch nicely.

Alan approached the old woman, he looked deeply at her.

The witch had long white hair, a long head and two big green eyes. You could also see in her mouth that she had lost half of her teeth.

"My grandaughter needs a family which could take good care of her, a friend with whom she could play with. She almost doesn't play and works all the time under the pressure of your daughter Kirsty! I would like to find someone in her mother's family. You see, I cannot move," He showed off his wheelchair. "I am ninety-one years old. I can't even help her with the washing up. I am useless and I am angry with myself. Help me please! You know all and see all. Look if you could find someone, to make your daughter stop bullying Annie. Kirsty does not want Annie at the house and I must find a safe place for her. Not in the orphanage of course."

"My daughter does not speak to me anymore because of your son and she won't listen to me. You know, you can do something for your grandaughter and it is not..." She looked at his wheelchair. "It's not because you're paralysed that you cannot help her. I have just what's necessary to help you."

"Oh, Marvel! No conditions," said Alan while threatening her with his finger. "No conditions this time. You know that I cannot belong to you, I am old enough and I am tired. Tired of the quarrels between you and me, between our two families, I tire of it all."

The old woman looked at him while smiling.

"After having lived the life of a Parrot, the life of an Eagle and the life of a Vulture, you will belong to me." said the witch.

"What does that mean?" asked Alan.

"Since I wanted you for my husband, you still preferred to marry Carla, I always waited and here comes the moment to have you for myself. If you die under one of these forms, you will belong to me for eternity." shouted Marvel.

"What does that mean?" asked Alan once more.

The old woman cackled loudly and took out her magic wand she pointed it towards Alan.

"You believed that by coming here, you were going to find a solution for your problems? Slave Bird!" howled the old woman.

And Boom! A light similar to the flash of lightening sprung up in the house and Alan was transformed into a Parrot. The bird started to fly in the house in all directions under the amused glance of the old witch. She also transformed herself into a female Parrot and chased him, Alan found an open window and he fled into the night, the old witch lost sight of him in the dark.

Alan looked at his feet and they had become bird's legs, his body was covered with feathers. He extended his arms and saw that they had become wings with beautiful blue feathers. He wanted to speak and he noticed that he had in the place of his lips, a yellow beak. He wanted to move and he was carried by the wind.

"Oh, I can fly. I CAN FLY!" said a surprised Alan.

He had time to see from the sky, the house of the old witch it remained well lit. Something that the witch said played over and over in his head (you will have the life of a Parrot, the life of an Eagle, the life of a Vulture and you shall belong to me.) Alan felt light and was balanced by the wind. He flew away on the left, then on the right until he found how to control his body in the air. He looked around and saw a light coming far from the bottom. The Parrot tried to land and it perched on a window.

"I know this house, it is the Martins'!" said Alan.

The Parrot went further and recognised the park. He looked where to sit.

"Ardwick Green Park! The house, my house is not far," continued the Parrot. He took off and knocked his head against a tree. Alan now felt dizzy.

"Oh, my body! I don't have the body of a human anymore. My wheelchair, I don't have that anymore. I will go to my family and nobody will recognise me. Annie, my little dear sweet Annie, what will happen to her?"

The rain started to fall. Alan was saddened, he went to sit on a branch and felt water sticking on his body. He wasn't cold, a pleasant feeling took him. The blue Parrot shook its body to make the water fall to the ground below, as it had been stuck to his feathers. - After all, Alan thought, "I didn't die. Let's wait for the rising of the sun to decide what to do."

The Parrot opened his wings widely and covered himself with his feathers. He closed his eyes and did not feel anything anymore. Alan fell asleep.

"Ku- koo, kuk-kuk-kuk-oo" "Ku- koo, kuk-kuk-kuk-oo" "Ku- koo, kuk-kuk-kuk-oo"

The noise sounded so extremely close to his ears that Alan thought of Madge and Madeline squeaking the wheels of his wheelchair - "Ku-koo, kuk-kuk-kuk-oo" "Ku- koo, kuk-kuk-kuk-oo" "Ku- koo, kuk-kuk-kuk-oo"

Alan opened his eyes and discovered it was a mother Cuckoo that was feeding her children, close to him in her nest. The furious mother advanced towards him and tried to give him a peck with her beak. Alan dodged the blow and fled. The mother followed him and Alan flew further away. He went to settle on another branch, He was now in a park. Alan recognised the monument and the playground.

"Ardwick Green Park! I am in Ardwick Green Park," screamed the bird happily. Alan the Parrot looked around and saw a little girl sitting on a bench. She was crying. She was looking towards the sky.

"Annie! Oh, Annie!" said the Parrot after recognising her. "My little Annie."

He flew downwards and went to sit on a bench close to her. The noise of his legs on the bench made her raise her head. Annie looked at him and smiled. She approached the Parrot. She picked Alan up and kissed him on the head.

"Hello, Mister Parrot. You're so beautiful!" said Annie

"Hello little madam." stammered Alan.

Annie started to laugh and shook her head with delight.

"I am not a dame. I am a little girl and my name is Annie."

"Annie, Annie, Annie." stumbled Alan.

The Magic Parrot realised he could not talk as easily as a human.

Alan looked at Annie's face and saw that she had swollen eyes.

"Did you cry Annie?" asked the Parrot, his eyes rose towards her.

She looked at him sadly and wiped her eyes with her right hand.

"I did the washing! Mrs Kirsty said that I didn't! Madge and Madeline threw all the clothes in the mud so that I had to start it again.

When I don't manage to do the work, they punish me. I woke up this morning and Mister Grandfather had disappeared. He was the only family I had."

Alan remembered the scene of yesterday evening and he asked while going round in circles.

"Where is your mum, Annie?"

"I do not have a mother. Mister the dad of Madge and Madeline said to me that I am an orphan who was born in his stable and I must do all that Mrs Kirsty says to me or he will send me to the orphanage,"

She stopped one moment and she looked at the blue bird sadly. "What is the orphanage Mister Parrot?"

Alan wanted to speak and started to stammer. The bird rolled its tongue in its beak.

"The orphanage, the orphanage, the orphanage." stated Alan.

His body was bouncing as he spoke. He jumped and went to settle on another bench. Annie laughed at him; she followed him on the bench.

"Mister Parrot does not know what the orphanage means. Oh! Me either. I never went to school like Madge and Madeline. Their school is just on the other side of the park and I often watch the children playing during break time. I am also punished for that."

Annie moved towards the bird and took him in her arms. She noticed that he was wet and wiped the Parrot with her dress. She gave him a kiss on the head.

"Oh! You are wet. I imagine, your cage was opened and you escaped. Your dad and mum must be looking for you everywhere. You know Mister Parrot, do you believe that one day I will see my dad and my mum in Heaven?" asked Annie.

Alan looked at her without saying a word. The little girl cradled the bird and continued.

"I would like to have a dad and a mum like Madge and Madeline, to go to the school, even have a beautiful baby doll with long hair which I would comb."

Alan had tears in his eyes, he wanted to wipe them, but they did not run. He opened his wings and one feather glided against Annie's face.

He tickled her which made her laugh.

Alan saw her face illuminated with joy. He had never seen her like that.

A great happiness filled his heart, he wanted to speak, but no sound left his beak. He shook his body violently and regained the use of his tongue.

"Orphanage, orphanage, orphanage." screamed the bird.

Annie continued laughing more. She put him on a bench and started to dance around him.

"Orphanage, orphanage, orphanage." repeated the little girl imitating the Parrot.

Annie heard her name far off and went towards the house. She took her Parrot with her and she hid him under her dress. She went into the stable; she put the Parrot on the hay close to Russell the horse and left running towards the house.

"Where are you Annie?" exploded Kirsty.

Annie ran through the large gate and she fell on her stepmother who carried her with her two hands.

"No! No! No!" cried Annie.

Alan heard Annie screaming and his heart jumped in his chest, he flew towards the entrance of the stable. He saw Kristy dragging Annie like a small bag of flour towards the house and she threw her near Peter's feet.

"Here! She was wandering around the stable when she should be preparing the twins for school. She deserves to be punished. Peter, you must take her to the orphanage, far from here." said his wife.

"Darling, not today. I am worried about my father. How could he leave the house? What will I do now? I don't know where to look for him" said Peter, worriedly.

Kirsty put her two hands on her hips and tried to comfort her husband.

"You worry for an old man who wasn't worth it anymore. Instead of you worrying about his leaving, you should try to find where he hid the fortune. The gold coins of your mother Carla. I need them for my daughters." yelled his wife.

"Where do you believe I will find these gold coins? My father was a crafty one, a nasty old man who hid everything since the death of my mother. He didn't tell me, ever!" He turned towards Annie and he asked her.

"He said something to you, didn't he? He told you where he went, where he hid those gold coins? You will tell me girl!

Peter shook Annie violently; Alan could not bear it anymore, so he started to fly non-stop round Russell and scratched the horse's back causing it to get angry.

The horse neighed and Alan scratched him again with all his strength. Russell cut the rope, which held him then he bolted out the stable, furiously. Peter left Annie and ran after the horse. Annie took advantage of the situation and fled towards the house.

Alan went to sit on the kitchen window and found Annie there, all alone, doing the dishes. She jumped in fright because of the sound of Alan's wings on the window and broke a plate.

"Oh! I will be punished today," said Annie.

"Why Annie?" asked Alan.

"I am so clumsy, I broke a plate. And the punishment of the day will be..." moaned Annie,

Alan did not let her finish her sentence. He left the window and floated in front of the girl.

"No food for Annie, the smacking for Annie and what did Annie do wrong today?" mocked the Parrot.

She started to laugh while looking at him; she leaned towards him.

"How do you know this Mister Parrot?" asked the little girl.

"I am a Parrot which hears all and which sees all. Don't you worry my little beauty, nobody will touch anymore." Alan succeeded to say.

"I still broke a plate and Mrs Kirsty will see it when she goes in the kitchen," said Annie. The little girl stood up and imitated the accent of her stepmother; she posed with her hands on her hips. She started counting with her fingers. "The little orphan broke a plate, didn't dress the twins for school in time and didn't cook the meals. I will give her such a smack, which will send her to join her mother... "

"And her father." added the Parrot.

"How do you know that Mister Parrot?" asked Annie.

"I am a Parrot..." answered Alan.

"Which sees all and hears all," she said knowingly.

"Mister Parrot, if I learn how to pay attention, I will not break anymore plates, if I learn how to work quicker I…"

Alan flew and went in front of her again. He beat his wings frantically.

"Your age doesn't allow you to work quickly, to pay attention to every detail. You are only a baby." disapproved the Parrot.

"A baby! I am not a baby anymore; I am eight and half years old. Almost nine "exclaimed Annie while posing with her hands on the hips.

The little girl began to pout and started counting with her fingers proudly.

"I can sew; I can cut tomatoes and onions. I can comb my hair and those of the twins, which means I'm not a baby, Mister Parrot!"

"From now on my little Annie, your life will be like a song," said the Parrot as he started to sing. "Annie the little Princess covered with gold covered by gold."

"Oh! I know this song. It's my song! Madam Grandmother, Mrs Carla use to sing it all the time to me," said Annie who babbled.

"Annie the little Princess covered with gold, covered by gold. A beautiful little Princess rich in gold, rich in gold, when you grow up, you will see. Your life will be easier."

"Annie, the little Princess covered with gold, covered by gold." Alan sang the lullaby with her cheerfully.

"Mister Parrot, I am so unhappy, I lost Madam Grandmother and Mister Grandfather. I am alone in this world," said Annie sadly.

Alan wanted to cheer her up.

"Oh! You are not alone in the world. I am here and your life will be easier now I promise."

The bird flew away in the kitchen and spread its wings over the crockery that Annie was washing. Suddenly, all became clean. The little girl looked around the kitchen and was amazed to see the bird making miracles.

Alan flew into the living room and went into the rooms. Annie followed the Parrot everywhere in the house and noticed its work. It made everything shine in the house and glued the dish, which Annie had broken.

For once in his life, Alan was proud of himself. He launched a glance towards Annie and he saw she was astonished.

"How did you do that Mister Parrot? You help me like Mister Grandfather, he always helped me. He did the washing up as best he could, but he always tried to help me," said Annie.

Alan did not let her finish he came close to her. He strongly beat his wings to draw her attention.

"You loved him, Mister Grandfather?" asked Alan.

"Oh, yes! He was all that I valued in the world. You know what Mister Parrot, you made me happy today like Mister Grandfather," murmured Annie.

The Parrot wanted to laugh but no sound left its beak

Chapter 2 - A new home.

Madge ran after her sister. The twins were playing hide-and-seek. Madeline went to hide behind the small apple tree and heard her sister counting.

"One, two, three, and four..." counted Madge.

She knocked herself against the tree, which shook through the force. She saw a bird flying away and it went to sit on the roof then on the house's window.

"A Parrot... a blue Parrot!" shouted Madeline.

Her sister approached it and they both ran after the bird that then left the window and returned to the small tree. It flew branch to branch.

"Dad, dad! We found a Parrot." screamed the twins.

Peter ran after the Parrot and managed to catch it. He gave the bird to his daughters. Annie heard the echo of the screams behind the house. She went to see what was happening and saw the Parrot in the hands of Peter. She believed that he wanted to kill him.

"Mister Parrot, my Parrot," howled Annie with all her strength.

They all looked at Annie as if they were petrified of her. Madge and Madeline then started to scream.

"No, it is our Parrot. We found it. Dad, we found the Parrot, didn't we?"

"Yes, it is your Parrot. And Annie should not come near the bird." said Peter

"Yes, it is our Parrot and Annie should not come near the bird," repeated the twins.

A cage in the living room held Alan prisoner, he looked at Annie who sat alone on the large sofa and Alan moved in the cage, she raised her eyes towards him and smiled. He started to sing while beating his wings wildly.

"Annie the little Princess covered with gold covered by gold. Beautiful little Princess rich in gold, rich in gold. When you will grow up, you will see. Your life will be easier."

"Mister Parrot, everyone's gone. The Granger family went to the Zoo and I don't have the right to go near you they say. What will I do now?" asked Annie.

"You will do nothing. Sit there and relax!" ordered to the bird.

"My Parrot, I must do the washing up," said Annie

"No Annie, you will not do the washing up. I will do it and as soon as I finish, I will teach you how to read."

"Teach me how to read Mister Parrot? It is I, who should teach you how to read. Now after me, A-n-n-i-e."

"Annie!" repeated the Parrot abruptly.

Annie laughed as she left the sofa and went closer to the cage.

"To start, I must give you a name. I will call you Alan like after my grandfather.
Do you like the name Mister Parrot?"
"Yes, yes, yes. My name is Alan, My name is Alan." sang the bird while swinging itself from side to side in the cage.
He pointed his wings towards the door of the cage and the cage doors opened. He flew away on the left and on the right leaving the house clean and tidy once more.
"Alan, how do you do that?" asked Annie.
Alan flew in front of her and beat his wings while signing for her to follow him, the bird moved towards the library and with his beak, made the books fall. "A reading book, a Victorian novel, a book for mathematics and one for writing and spelling," counted the Parrot.
Suddenly, the Parrot channelled a blue light from his eyes towards the books, which then transported all knowledge of its content into Annie.
"Annie, you can read. Try!" said the bird while showing her the reading book.
Annie took the reading book in her hands and started to read. She read a whole page and looked at the Parrot.
"Alan, I can read, I can read." screamed the little girl excitedly.
She howled so happily. Annie put the book down and started to dance in the living room.

Tired of this she picked up the Parrot in her arms to give him a cuddle then she went to lie on the sofa and swiftly fell fast asleep.

Kristy opened the door of the house. She found Annie sleeping on the sofa, the Parrot locked up in its cage. She threw a glance in the house. All was clean and tidy. She widened her eyes in surprise while she approached the little girl.
"Annie! You're always sleeping! Have you cooked the meal for my daughters?" shouted Kirsty in the little girl's ear.
Annie woke up abruptly. Kirsty went in the kitchen and saw the well drawn up table with the cooked meals. The pots were washed and placed in the cupboard wall. The twins ran in the kitchen and went to sit down on the table.
"Mum, mum the meals are ready," said Madge.
Kirsty took Annie along to the kitchen and showed her the room.
"Who helped you to do the housework? Who cooked the meal? Do you think that you will escape from your punishment? Who helped you to clean the house?" asked her stepmother.
Before Annie could even open her mouth, Alan leapt from his cage and flew towards Kirsty's head and scratched her with all his strength.
The woman started to howl and left the house running. Alan continued to scratch her until the arrival of Peter who chased the bird with a stick.
Alan went to sit on the window of the stable, but Peter followed him again.

He flew away again and went to perch on a branch in the local park. He looked while Peter cursed and went back towards the house. Annie remained in the house this time, but for once was not punished.

"Someone came here and did the washing up. Someone cooked the meal and I want to know who!" demanded bruised Kirsty.

"If it is someone, that is good for us." replied Peter.

"And if it is your father?" asked Kirsty.

"Oh, My Father! You know that he can't stand up anymore."

"Then, it could be Annie's mother's family," rumbled Kirsty

"Annie does not have a family. She was born in my stable, off a woman whom did not have anything on her, no paper, or an identity card," added Peter

"How could someone do everything and so quickly?" Asked Kirsty

Peter defended Annie for the very first time. He replied angrily.

"Annie was fast, that is all and she has obeyed you for once in her life!"

Annie could not believe her ears. She looked at them arguing. Peter had defended her in front of his wife. Annie stood up and entered the kitchen. She took some seeds, put them in her pocket and left the house. She went in the stable looking for the Parrot. She found Russell and his two foals.

25

The little girl looked for the bird with her bright little eyes, but could not find him so she started to cry. She went near Russell the horse.

"Russell, have you seen my blue Parrot? I want to give him some seeds," asked Annie to the horse.

Russell looked at Annie sadly and gave her a friendly nudge on her head. The horse neighed and raised its back legs. The little girl cried more now. She went towards Russell's foals.

"Jim and Jam, have you seen my Parrot? Have you seen him? Oh, I can't believe I've lost the only friend I had!" cried Annie.

Alan felt like a tear was running from his eye. He raised a wing and touched his face, but there was nothing. He thought that he could hear someone crying. He moved from one branch to another and saw Annie far off. The Parrot flew towards her; it entered the stable and sat close to her.

"Annie, why are you crying?" Asked Alan promptly.

"Oh, Mister Parrot! I thought that I lost you," screamed Annie.

"Annie, you will never lose me! Never!" said the bird.

Annie smiled. She picked up the Parrot and went towards the stable doors.

"Even when I grow old like Madam Carla? You will not leave me, will you? You Promise?" asked Annie

"When you grow old like Mrs Carla, I will have passed on, but I will not leave you. I won't, I promise." swore Alan.

She took the seeds out her pocket and put them in the palm of her hand. Alan pecked away hungrily at the seeds.

"Now, you need some water. We are going back to the house and I will get some water for you in the kitchen," said Annie.

She hid the Parrot under her dress and went in the kitchen. The little girl took a plate; she poured the water on it and positioned the Parrot on the table. She gave the water to Alan and he started to drink.

Annie went to the living room to see if anyone was there, she did not see anybody. She put the bird on her shoulder and went to her room. She put the bird beside the bedside lamp and gave him a kiss on the head then she lay very still on her mattress.

"Dad, dad." Annie heard from her room.

"There is a Parrot in my room..." shouted Madge to her father.

Peter went into the room and discovered a Parrot wedged behind the curtain. The bird had a broken leg and a broken wing.

"Dad, can I keep it?" asked Madge.

"No, you can't because your sister's Parrot attacked your mother.

First, let's see whether it is the same Parrot." answered Peter.

Annie woke up and saw Alan near her. She was relieved and took the bird in her arms and kissed him, in a reassured manner.

"Alan, my Parrot! We have a guest," said Annie.

Alan opened his eyes, jumped up and down while shaking his head.

"Another Parrot. Another Parrot." screamed the bird as it took refuge in Annie's arms.

"Marvel!" screamed the bird.

"Marvel. Who is Marvel?" asked Annie, confusedly.

The Parrot did not say a word; He flew nervously in the small room. Annie opened the door and they left the room. Alan fled to the window as soon as they reached the living room.

Alan was flying above the small apple tree when he heard Peter confirming.

"It's a female Parrot! It's a female Parrot!"

"Dad, let me keep it. Oh! Dad, I want to keep it," said Madge still very excited by the new arrival.

"First we need to take care of her broken leg, broken wing and to give her some food. Furthermore, your mother must give her blessing so that you can keep her," explained Peter.

Already, Madge ran towards Kirsty who had left the house followed by Madeline. "Mum, mum I found another Parrot in our room." said Madge.

Kirsty looked at the bird furiously and the little girl was not surprised by her mother's answer.

"No, not another bird in my house." scolded Kirsty.

"No, no, no!" Yelled Madge as she started to cry, Peter went in front of his wife; he knelt on the floor and begged her. He made a strange shape with his mouth, which made his two daughters laugh.

"You don't have to worry, it's a female Parrot." begged Peter.

"I don't care. I don't want another Parrot in my house! These birds should be wild and free, but not free enough to attack me and I have better things to do than discussing this trivia. Annie, where is Annie?" Kirsty blasted.

Madge threw herself to the ground and started to wail. One moment afterwards, Madeline did the same; their parents looked at them with wonder. Marvel looked at the scene with much amusement and went to sit on Madge's knees. The female Parrot opened her wings largely and spread a smoke that calmed the group.

Kirsty took the Parrot in her arms and gave her a kiss on the head Peter did the same. The parents caressed the bird with their hands.

"Mum, Dad, can we keep her?" begged the twins.

Kirsty agreed. She went to put the Parrot in the cage reserved for Alan.

"You're not like the other Parrot. I have the impression that you are well mannered," said Kirsty. "Eh, girls! We must give the bird a name."

Marvel beat her wings in the cage. Kirsty bent her head towards the cage and heard the Parrot murmuring.

"Kirsty, I am Marvel your mother," said the female Parrot.

The woman opened her eyes largely and closed them again quickly. She heard her daughters coming near them. The twins approached the cage and Madge put a finger in one of the holes.

"We will give you a beautiful name. I hope that you are well mannered," said Madge

"You are well mannered, aren't you my Parrot?" Asked Madeline.

"Yes, I am well mannered, I am polite and I don't scratch. I don't swear and I don't do silly things," answered Marvel.

Kirsty moved her daughters from the cage, still in shock and called her husband who ran with a glass of juice in his hand.

"Peter, listen to this. The Parrot said that..." Said Kirsty.

"Listen to what?" asked Peter close to the cage.

"I am well mannered, I am polite and I don't scratch. I don't swear and I don't do silly things," continued the blue Parrot.

Peter laughed and took Marvel out of the cage and kissed the bird on the head.

"This is the ideal pet for our twins. If you do not swear, don't do silly things, we will keep you forever." said Peter, happily.

"Don't you agree children, why don't we call the Parrot Marvel?" Kirsty suggested cautiously.

"Marvel like your mum." Peter said.

"Marvel, like our grandmother?" asked the twins at the same time.

"Yes! Marvel like your grandmother." nervously replied their mother.

Peter put Marvel in the cage and went to the kitchen. He took some seeds and fruits, giving them to the Parrot. He closed the cage again, then took his wife by the hips and simultaneously kissed her on her cheeks.

Annie was watching all of this by the stairs. The couple passed near to her and Kirsty looked down to Annie. Peter laughed after touching his wife's cheek.

"What are you staring at? Get to work." yelled Kirsty.

Annie stood up straight, fearing to be punished again.

"Get to work!" said the twins, imitating their mother.

"Annie, first make a bandage for the twin's Parrot." ordered Peter.

"Yes Sir." answered Annie.

"Yes Sir." repeated the twins mockingly.

Annie opened the cage and picked Marvel up. She went in the kitchen and climbed on the chair, she took the first aid box from a small cupboard fixed on the wall. She sat down and gently made a bandage for the Parrot's leg as well as her wing.

Alan hid behind the curtain of the living room. He was contemplating Kirsty and Marvel pretending not to know each other. The girls sat close to the fireplace. It was Saturday and it was raining outside.

Annie sat on her own with instructions not to disturb the twins. Alan looked at her sadly. Annie's red cheeks swelled and her eyes were filled with anger. She had her legs stretched on the ground with her arms crossed over her chest.

Alan approached her without showing himself; He tickled her with one of his feathers while making a sign to the little girl to leave the house. Annie suddenly saw the Parrot and started to laugh. Everyone looked at her.

"Why are you so excited, Annie?" asked Kirsty.

Annie did not say a word, but laughed again after looking at the Parrot. She had now irritated Kirsty and the twins. Madge approached Annie and gave her a smack on her head.

"Annie, stop making fun of me!" shouted Madge.

Annie continued to laugh and Madge shouted again. "Naughty girl, didn't you hear what I just said?"

"Oh, I wasn't making fun of you," claimed Annie.

"Oh, yes you were!" Madge answered back.

"Annie, you're naughty! You are teasing Madge. I saw you looking at the leg of her doll. You sewed his foot badly," said Madeline in turn.

"You sewed my doll's foot badly and you were laughing at me. It's because you don't have your own," added Madge while showing her tongue.
Annie defended herself.
"No, it is not true."
The atmosphere became unbearable so Kristy came to the aid of her daughters.
"Annie, Go to the kitchen!" said the woman.
Marvel, who was now hopping in the cage, imitated Kirsty. The woman started to laugh, loudly.
"Annie, Go to the kitchen! Annie, Go the kitchen!" sang the female Parrot.
The twins started laughing. Their mother went to play with the blue bird in the cage.

Kirsty was excited. She opened the cage and freed the bird, which flew away to follow Annie who went into the kitchen.
Annie entered the kitchen, leaving the mother and her daughters in the living room. She went to hide behind the door. She saw Alan, by a small hole as she was behind the door. He was flying behind the curtain near the kitchen window when the little girl came towards him and took him in her arms.
"Annie, how are you doing?" Asked Alan.
"I'm fine, thank you." answered the little girl as she swallowed her tears.
"You aren't fine, I saw you crying," added Alan.

"Yes, you saw me crying. I cry everyday Mister Parrot. I miss not having my mother, a family," said Annie.

The male Parrot comforted her.

"Thinking so much about your mother will not bring her back. Don't worry about her, my little Annie."

"And my dad! Alan, do you believe that I will see them one day? Could the life in the orphanage be better than here?" asked the little girl.

"You're not well treated here and it will be the same at the orphanage. Don't be upset because of Marvel's words." replied the bird.

"Oh! I'm not upset. Marvel is a Parrot and like all Parrots, she repeats the words of everyone. I believe that she is a good bird, like you Alan," affirmed Annie.

"Oh, oh, oh, not like me." screamed Alan leaving her arms.

"And why wouldn't you two like to know each other. We will wait when the house is asleep, you will say hello to her." suggested Annie.

"Oh, no, no no no." refused Alan as he shook his head.

Alan and Annie heard steps coming towards them. They hid behind the door. Kirsty entered the kitchen accompanied by her daughters and Marvel the bird; it perched on the cupboard stuck to the wall. The female Parrot saw Alan behind the door and started to beat her wings savagely.

"A Parrot, a Parrot, a Parrot." shouted Marvel.

Kirsty moved towards the door, she found Annie and Alan. She tried to catch the bird, which fled to the living room, Marvel closely behind him.

"The beastly Parrot was hiding in the kitchen," howled Kirsty.

"The beastly Parrot, wicked Parrot," screamed Marvel while trying to catch Alan.

The twins ran after Alan, he tried to escape, but they closed all the doors and windows in the house. Kirsty caught him finally. Alan was locked up in the cage with Marvel.

"The beastly Parrot! Wicked Parrot!" shouted the female Parrot cheerfully.

Alan went to settle in a corner of the cage ready to defend himself. Marvel tried to approach him and he started to beat his wings. The noise of the wings attracted the girls and they gathered in front of the cage.

"I want to get marry! I want to get marry!" screamed Marvel.

Alan continued to beat his wings and the girls made fun of him. Madge put her hand in the cage and pushed Alan towards Marvel. The birds collided and Alan tried to fly out of the cage, but the cage was bewitched and would not open.

"I don't want to get married! I don't want to get married!" howled the male Parrot surprised by the request of the witch.

Madge pushed Alan backwards towards Marvel; this caused him to fall to bottom of the cage and become attached to Marvel's leg.

The twins looked at the two birds with satisfaction, they then went to bed.

Alan looked at Annie, as she was the last to leave. He gazed at her with a glance that was full of grief. The little girl shrugged her shoulders, desperately unhappy that she was unable to help him; she left and entered her room. Alan heard Annie closing the small door.

The house was calm and asleep. Marvel opened the door of the cage and left; she transformed herself into an old woman. She stood in front of the cage, with her hands on the hips.

"And like that, Alan doesn't want to get married!" Shouted the witch.

"And why would I?" rumbled Alan.

"Quite simply because you belong to me!" Answered Marvel with certainty.

"Oh, I don't belong to you!" objected Alan.

The old woman laughed wholeheartedly and took her long white hair in her hands and made a French pleat.

"You don't belong to me! You came to my home asking for my help." began the old woman.

"The help was for my grandaughter, not to marry you," scolded the Parrot.

"Ah! The help for your grandaughter! You have given her this help already, you do the washing up, and you clean the house. You used my power very well so far that I can see." Admitted Marvel.

"What I give to her is not good enough. I must find a member of her family so she can leave this house." said Alan.

"A member of her family! Her family is here, her father, her half-sisters and her stepmother. And it is for this reason only I sent her mother to die here!" continued the old woman.

"Ah! You knew Annie's mother?" enquired Alan.

Marvel smiled and put a finger in the cage. Alan went backwards to corner of the cage, ready to bite.

"I know everything you have done for generations. For generations, I have lived; I know all of your misfortunes and your joys. I have made you pay sometimes because you chose Carla over Me." murmured the witch.

"What did you do to make me pay? By entering your house that night, I allowed you to enter my life again. Marvel, I am only an old man and I cannot be a woman's husband anymore." announced Alan.

"You will live the life of a Parrot, the life of an Eagle, the life of a Vulture and you will belong to me," said Marvel.

She transformed herself again, but into a squirrel this time, she opened the door and left the house.

Alan left the cage and flew nervously into the living room, as well as the kitchen and cleaned it all. He was questioning himself about the witch's choice words. He opened the door of Annie's bedroom and saw her sleeping deeply. She was breathing strangely.

The Parrot returned to his cage; he entered and folded his legs. He closed his eyes and thought about Carla, his late wife as he fell asleep.

Noises coming from the backyard awoke Alan. He opened his eyes and shook his head.
He looked into the cage and saw Marvel asleep close to him. The cage was open and he snuck out, he flew in the living room, then into the kitchen searching for Annie.
He saw her by the window outside. She was making flower bouquets in the garden. Alan went to sit on the small apple tree and Annie saw him. The little girl smiled to him.
"Oh, Marvel's fiancé! Are you ready for the wedding?" joked Annie.
"No, I won't get married, I won't get married." objected Alan, furious at the preparation of his wedding.
The furious bird did not stop repeating the sentence and Annie tried to catch him to calm him down. The blue Parrot came close to her when he was calmer. Annie took him in her hand and placed her finger on his beak reassuring him.
"Don't be scared, Marvel is not going to eat you. I think that she will make you happy and you will have a big family. The twin's dad is very happy with Mrs Kirsty. And you know what; there are beautiful seeds and juicy fruits, as well as some nuts for you both."
"I don't want to get marry! I don't want to get marry!" continued Alan.

Annie burst into laughter. She ran towards Madge and Madeline. The girls had prepared a small table on which they had put seeds, fruits and some ice-cold water. Kirsty brought the cage where Marvel was and put it on the table. Peter came close to the table with a glass of water to hand.

"A wedding, so very early in the morning! See I already drink a toast to the groom. And you, Marvel, promise me to make this nasty, wild, spiteful Parrot into a model husband, especially a good father to your future children!" pronounced Peter.

Annie put Alan on the table. The bird started to hop while turning around.

"Annie, Annie my little Princess covered by gold. I don't want to get married," begged Alan.

"Give me a reason! Give me one reason," demanded Annie as she bent towards him. "I don't like this female Parrot. I don't like Marvel," answered the male Parrot with an almost strained voice.

"I love Alan. I want to marry him. I want to marry. I want to marry," repeated Marvel.

Annie picked up the male Parrot in her hands and took him along to the bottom of the garden. She gave him a kiss on the head and opened her two hands. She released Alan who flew away. He went to sit on a far away fence.

"Annie, why did you let him escape?" asked Kirsty in anger.

"Naughty Annie, naughty Annie, naughty Annie." howled Marvel, furious to see Alan leave.
Marvel left the cage and tried to scratch Annie. Peter barred the road to the female Parrot. He caught Marvel and put her back in the cage. He closed the small doors to the cage carefully.

Alan flew further from the house at great speed.
"He disappeared in the sky. We won't see him anymore," said Peter to his wife.
"It's Annie's fault. She let him escape. Oh, she must be punished. Peter, why did you put Marvel back in the cage? She must avenge herself!" said the furious woman.
"It's not because I love Annie that I will not let her be bitten by a bird. It's just wrong!" shouted Peter as he stopped his wife from releasing the female Parrot.
Annie lowered her head slightly and started to cry silently while looking at Peter. The twins were running wildly here and there in the garden.

Alan went to sit on the branch of a tree in the local park. He heard horrible cries coming from the house. He returned near the house and sat on the fence.
"Annie stole the gold coins, Annie stole the gold coins," shouted Marvel suddenly.
Kirsty ran after Annie, she caught her and held her firmly.

Peter wanted to prevent his wife smacking Annie and he received a punch to the face. Kirsty opened the cage and took Marvel on her other hand.

"Mother, did you see Annie take the gold coins?" asked Kirsty.

"Since when is the Parrot your mother?" shouted Peter.

"She hid them under her mattress." answered Marvel.

The female Parrot flew in the house then entered the small room followed by Peter, Kirsty and the twins.

Peter grabbed his wife by the hand.

"You can't be sure. How could Annie know where my father had hidden them?" began Peter as he defended Annie.

"Out of my sight!" ordered Kirsty as she pushed her husband away.

She lifted the mattress and found a small bag.

"You still defend her, you always defend her these days just like that father of yours. You don't love us!" howled Kirsty.

She took the small bag and showed it to Peter; he took the bag while looking at Annie.

"What was this small bag doing under her mattress?" bellowed Kirsty.

Peter stood in front of his wife with the small bag while Annie was behind him, she was crying louder now. Madge and Madeline bit their father on his hand and he moaned in pain.

The small bag fell on the floor and Annie picked it up. She took the bag and put it in her hands behind her back. Kirsty ran towards Annie in the living room and took the bag of gold coins.

Alan felt himself fill with anger. He heard Annie screaming; he opened his wings and flew towards the door of the house.

As Alan flew towards the house, his wings got larger and thicker; he was rapidly changing into the form of an Eagle, a big Golden Eagle.

He entered the house speedily; Alan grabbed the small bag from Kirsty's hands with his beak. He took Annie, by her trousers and her hand, in his powerful claws and left the house. He performed this rescue like a flash of lightening hitting an object.

He heard Peter and Kirsty shouting far off. He looked at the little girl and saw that she had fainted through all the excitement.

Happily, Alan moved towards the clouds.

He made sure that he held Annie tightly.

They then soared higher and higher in the sky and disappeared.

Chapter 3 - Graceland.

Alan looked at his powerful wings splitting through the wind. He looked at his claws and saw that they had a good grip of Annie. He flew for hours upon hours.

He wanted to land and threw a glimpse below; he saw a large forest that seemed endless.

"Where am I?" Alan asked himself after he discarded the small bag full of gold on the ground.

The big Eagle went down and softly placed Annie on some flat earth. He looked all around himself and saw every kind of tree surrounding the area. He came close to Annie and with his beak, he touched her, she seemed to be recovering slowly this made him less worried; he turned away from Annie with a lighter heart.

Alan went to pick up the small bag from where it had fallen and put it beside the little girl. He opened the bag with his beak without awaking Annie and he saw the gold coins.

"Marvel, you old witch! You had a very good trap," continued Alan. He thought now that Marvel found where he had hidden the gold coins; she then had stashed them and placed them in Annie's room. She would have used this to blackmail him if he did not marry her; Alan smiled at himself proudly for avoiding this trap.

Alan tightened himself against Annie's body.

He started to comb his feathers on his body with his beak; he was now a dark brown colour like most Golden Eagles but a lot bigger.

Annie was still sleeping, she had been for hours and Alan was now anxious. He currently thought of what he could do to take the shape of a Parrot again.

He walked around between the trees to help with his thinking; he came back without success. Alan opened his wings boldly and beat them wildly. He felt Annie moving and came closer to her. Annie awoke and sat up. She looked around herself anxiously.

"Mister Parrot, where are we?" asked the troubled little girl.

Alan watched his body as it became tiny again; he now knew how to control the shape of the Parrot as long as he was calm he could keep control.

"We are in a big forest, I don't know where!" replied the Parrot

"Oh, Alan! I ruined your wedding by letting you go." continued Annie, angrily.

"You saved my life actually." reassured the bird.

"Saved your life? You didn't like Marvel that much, Mister Parrot?" asked the little girl again.

"Like her! I hated her. Furthermore, she was overweight like an old, rusty pan," protested Alan.

"But Alan, you could have been happy." said Annie smiling.

The Parrot started hopping and he climbed on Annie's knees. She looked at him with amusement; Alan went down again and started walking around.

"No, no, no. Marvel is not my type of bird," laughed the Parrot.

Annie stood up and walked with him. She picked Alan up in her arms and gave him a cuddle.

"I don't even know how we got here. This isn't the problem. The problem is to see how we get out of here. We need help. Let's go, Alan," suggested Annie.

She put Alan on her right shoulder and continued to walk. Annie walked for hours and she did not see any houses. She sat down beside a tree, due to her tiredness.

"Alan, we're lost. What are we going to do?" worried Annie.

"Don't lose hope. Wait here." said the Parrot.

Alan flew away and left Annie seated close to the tree. He flew for miles and miles, he saw nothing, but a green sea of trees.

Annie heard a noise coming from the trees and looked around. She saw a bird falling, followed by a big Eagle with a red neck. He had brown feathers, two big eyes like those of an owl, yellow legs and a pointed-razor sharp beak. The flamboyant Ornate Hawk-Eagle was a chasing a Jamaican Woodpecker. Annie stood up and looked for a stick.

The little girl ran up behind and struck the Eagle, which then turned towards her. He opened his large wings and tried to bite her. The bird ran towards Annie and she screamed in fear. She shouted so loudly that Alan heard her voice and feared the worst.

Without knowing what was happening, Alan turned around and flew back all in one motion. As he arrived towards the ground, he became a Golden Eagle.

Alan landed on the Ornate Hawk- Eagle and tore some of his feathers off with a violent jab of his beak. The Ornate Hawk- Eagle attacked Alan and the two birds fought savagely. Alan took the helpless Ornate Hawk- Eagle in his claws and sent him crashing against a tree.

The Ornate Hawk- Eagle got back on his legs and opened his wings as he stared at Alan,

The Golden Eagle recognised the gleam in the eyes of the other Eagle.

"Marvel!" muttered Alan as he prepared to leap.

Alan flew towards and collided with the evil bird. Annie could no longer stand watching the two birds; with the stick to hand, she struck the big Ornate Hawk- Eagle.

The big bird left Alan and went towards the little girl. Annie gave him another strike, which dazed the creature; Alan took off and positioned his two powerful claws on the birds' head. He stuck him on the ground to restrain him. Alan gave him wild pecks with his beak on his head the Ornate Hawk- Eagle was beaten.

"Powerful Eagle, don't kill him." begged Annie.
Alan turned round and looked at Annie. He moved away from the bird, which fled quickly. The little girl ran behind the Ornate Hawk- Eagle as it flew away injured. Alan opened his wings, which spanned most of the surrounding area and transformed himself into a Parrot once more.

"Annie! Annie!" Alan shouted worriedly.
The little girl came running towards him. She sat down and took him in her arms. Alan had felt that he had become a Parrot again. He looked at Annie who spoke to him breathlessly.
"Alan, I was attacked by this Eagle with a red neck; he wanted to kill a small bird. And then another big brown Eagle came to help me."
Annie looked around and saw the Jamaican Woodpecker. She took him and placed him close to the Parrot. She ripped the hem of her dress and bandaged the small bird. She looked at Alan, inspected his body and saw some traces of blood on his feathers.
"You are also wounded, Mister Parrot." She declared.
Annie hugged him and made a bandage for his left wing. She sat down with the two birds close to her.
"We haven't left the forest yet. How will we get home?" asked Annie, anxiously.
"My village, my city is not far from here," said a voice.

"Is your village near here Alan?" asked Annie while looking at him.

"No! I didn't speak," answered Alan.

They both looked at the Woodpecker, which inflated his feathers and shook his body.

"My village is near here. The City of the Birds is near here "repeated the Jamaican Woodpecker.

"You speak as well! What is your name? Where are you from?" asked Annie to the Woodpecker.

She saluted him as she gave him her other hand. The Woodpecker greeted her by tightening her hand under his wing. Annie took the wing and shook it firmly.

"Marty, my name is Marty and I am a Jamaican Woodpecker and I come from this forest." answered the Woodpecker politely.

The little girl looked at the bird. He had yellow feathers and behind those were ebony coloured feathers.

The back of his head was red and the front was white, his beak was so pointed that Annie playfully mocked it. She tightened her mouth so not to make it obvious, but then she started laughing.

"Marty, my name is Annie and here is my Parrot Alan. Where is your village?" she asked

"Near here." pointed Marty with his uninjured wing.

"Let's go. I'm hungry and I want to sleep. And then, I must look after you properly." continued Annie.

The Woodpecker went to the front of a tree and stroked the trunk with his beak as he emitting sounds.

"Toc-toc-toc-toc."

"What are you doing Marty?" asked Annie.

"I'm sending a message to my friends in the city." replied Marty.

"Toc-toc-toc-toc." "Toc-toc-toc-toc." they heard back.

"They're waiting for us!" shouted Marty.

The Woodpecker flew away in the forest followed by the Parrot. They took a different direction as Annie pressed on by foot trying desperately to keep up with them.

She looked at them flying as she walked and became annoyed.

"Hey, wait for me! I don't have wings to fly remember!" Shouted the furious little girl.

The birds returned towards her and they hovered slowly ahead on the road making it easier for Annie to walk to their speed. They arrived in a glade where they saw some large trees on which all kinds of large nests were perched. Marty turned all around the little girl who did well to dodge his long beak.

"I present to you the village of all Birds. The Central Glade, a small City of Graceland." said the Woodpecker proudly.

"But Marty there is nobody here," exclaimed Annie.

"Toc-Toc, we're here," continued Marty as he sat on the ground.

Nothing moved. The Woodpecker flew between some trees.

"Nothing!" He said turning to them in quite a perplexed state.

"I feel them. They all hid from us," said Alan.

"Hey! We're here," shouted Marty.

They heard noises from between the trees. Annie looked towards the sky and birds of all kinds started to fly towards them.

The Hummingbird beat their wings happily. The Cuckoos emitted a cuckoo meaning welcome. A large bird sat on the ground close to Annie. He looked at her strangely.

"What is your name?" Asked the Shoebill Stork.

Annie looked at his long yellow feather in the shape of a horn placed on his head. She leaned her head forward in a somewhat submissive manner

"Annie, my name is Annie. And you, what is your name? What do you have on your head?" answered Annie still quite amazed.

"My name is Bill and I am a Shoebill Stork, the King of the Birds. I took over the duties temporarily since Tom our king was made a prisoner," continued the large bird.

Annie did nothing but look at his head in amazement. She approached and touched the long feather.

"What you see on my head is a crown," added the Shoebill Stork.

"Ah, no! It is not a crown. That looks like a banana leaf yellowed in the sun. Wait, I will make you a good crown," boasted the little girl.

Marty came close to Bill who had just seen his crown removed from his head. Annie peered at his head, which resembled a Whale's head.

"You shouldn't be worried about Tom, he isn't dead. He is there in front of you," proclaimed Marty.

"Oh! Where is Tom?" asked the assembly of birds.

"Where is Tom?" asked Bill.

"There!" answered Marty promptly while pointing at Alan.

"Ah, no! I am not Tom. My name is Alan," said the Parrot surprised by the words of the Woodpecker. "Hello, my name is Alan."

A great silence settled. The birds stopped beating their wings. Some birds sat on the branches, others on the ground. They looked at the Parrot without understanding his words.

"Hey everyone, I am Alan." continued Alan.

"No, you are Tom. I watched you, a Golden Eagle, fighting against Mortal the evil Ornate Hawk-Eagle then transform yourself into a Parrot." stammered the Jamaican Woodpecker.

"Mortal! He fought against Mortal?" Asked the excited assembly.

Alan flew and went in front of Annie who had an astonished look. She looked perplexed. She opened her eyes widely.

"Annie," begged Alan "Tell them that I am Alan the Parrot and not an Eagle."
Annie defended him.
"Alan is a Parrot and he's just my Parrot."
"I watched you transform yourself into a Parrot after having overcome Mortal." began Marty while jumping on his two legs.
"Alan, you never told me that you could change your appearance?" exclaimed Annie.
Alan acknowledged this while turning around.
"I know some small tricks, but that does not make me their king. I am not Tom."
A Reeve's Pheasant went to sit close to Alan.
"Tell us if you are our Tom because we need him back, Mortal terrorises us and we need somebody who can defend us and destroy him. He killed almost all the Falcons, the Swans, the Swallows and Parrots of the jungle," said the Reeve's Pheasant.
"Have pity on us! I went to the Parrots. Most of them are dead," added a dove.
"If I was your king, I would avenge all of you for the other dead birds, let us see. Lead me into your forest." said Alan to the assembly.
The birds flew away leaving Annie alone on the spot. Marty beckoned to the little girl to follow them, but she would not move an inch. She started to shout instead.
"Oh, oh wait for me!"
Alan turned round and looked at her. He went back towards Annie and transformed himself into an enormous Golden Eagle.

"Climb up on my back!" said Alan.

Annie went up on his back, she firmly seized his neck and Alan flew away.

"Alan, how do you do that?" asked Annie in the air.

Alan did not answer but was in a hurry to catch up with the others. He recognised Marty in the crowd and went towards the Jamaican Woodpecker.

Alan, the Golden Eagle, flew over the jungle with Marty by his side. They were being followed by a whole colony of birds. They heard the cries of distress coming from the ground. Alan split through the wind once more to accelerate his descent.

He landed on a large glade to discover Mortal who was tearing the flesh off a dead Parrot. Annie went down from his back and sprung behind Alan. The two Eagles began to fight savagely.

The birds all sat on the branches watching the combat of the Eagles. Annie walked around the two Eagles.

"Alan! Go ahead beat him. Alan you can do it, beat him," shouted the little girl.

After several blows and clashing of claws, Alan seized Mortal's neck and managed to pin the bird on the ground. This time, He held firmly, letting Mortal beat his wings as a sign of defeat. Alan turned his claws; he twisted the neck of Mortal who expired.

"Yippy, yippy!" shouted Annie.

The birds left the branches and whirled around Alan.

"Alan, you're the best. You did it Alan, you did it!" Howled Annie while joining the birds.

She approached Alan and gave him a kiss on the head. All the birds walked round them; Bill came close to the Golden Eagle to congratulate him.

"Tom, you did it."

Alan beat his wings and walked over majestically towards Bill. He looked at him nervously.

"I am not Tom. My name is Alan!" growled Alan.

"Let's celebrate our new king!" screamed Marty with the other birds while flying over them. The crowd of birds sang while celebrating.

"Mortal is dead! Mortal is dead! Mortal is dead!"

Alan went towards the body of Mortal and moved it with his beak. He saw that the Ornate Hawk- Eagle had died; he twisted the body of the bird to make certain. Alan beat his wings in joy and to show his power.

"He is no more. Your enemy is dead!" said Alan to the crowd of birds, which in turn emitted cries of joy.

Annie put herself in the middle of the crowd and tried to calm the birds. Nobody heard her speaking. She moved towards the Whale-headed Stork who stopped dancing on his long legs.

"Bill! Hey, I'm hungry and thirsty," shouted the little girl close to his ears.

Bill hushed the assembly with a growl. The noise coming from his throat amused Annie.

"How did you do that?" asked Annie by imitating the growl.

Bill inflated his throat and pushed the air out to make the strange noise again. The little girl started to laugh. Annie twisted herself while laughing she was followed by the assembly of birds.

"I am delighted that amuses you, but we must find you something to eat and more importantly find you a place to sleep." said Bill.

The Shoebill Stork turned to the crowd and looked towards the trees.

"My dear friends, we have a beautiful Princess amongst us and we must please her.

We will build a large nest for her in the middle of the glade and will gather all the good food which we have in our forest," said Bill as he beat his wings. "Go, birds! Build a beautiful nest for Annie."

Bill voiced the strange noise once more; the birds then nervously scattered.

The Frigate Birds built the nest, by cutting broad leaves of the trees that they positioned on the ground.

Herons and the Ibises assembled four walls all around the leaves and the Long-Tailed Tailorbirds sewed the leaves between them.

Annie watched the birds building a beautiful hut between four trees and making a door with windows. Annie was happy with their work.

"My hut is finished and now, I'm hungry!" admitted Annie.

The Swans brought her beautiful mangos. Two Woodpeckers held a leaf by the two ends filled with water they gave it to Annie. The hummingbirds put themselves in a row and sang after Alan taught them the song of the Princess.

Annie laughed while looking at them. They made a harmonious noise. She ate fruits and kept some of them for Alan while he spoke with Bill.

"Thank you for defeating Mortal. Mortal destroyed most of the birds of prey that fought for our cause."

"When we saw that Mortal had arrested Tom, we said to ourselves that this is the end for the birds of the community," added a Pigeon.

"I couldn't even go to the river Loisa with my wife and children." said a Duck.

"We couldn't eat the fish of the rivers anymore. Praise the Gods! Mortal is dead." added a White Pelican as he put his wing on the back of his wife.

Annie left her hut and went towards them. She knelt close to the Pelicans. "Where is this river? I want to take a bath," asked Annie.

"My Princess, don't worry. My Kin and I will bring some water everyday so you can wash yourself. Wait and see!" proposed a Brown Pelican.

He flew away followed by many other Pelicans and they went towards the river. They drew water by their beaks and their throats inflated like large balloons. They returned towards the glade then poured water on the little girl. She started to dance on the spot. She rubbed her body.

Annie took off her dress to give it to a Swan who put the dress over a branch of a tree. She covered herself with two large leaves. The Ashy Tailorbirds sewed the leaves and made a beautiful small dress for Annie.

"That's it, I'm clean and I ate well. I'm going to bed now," proclaimed Annie as she looked at herself.

The birds pulled Annie by the arms towards the hut and she lay down on a large leaf. They covered her with another she was then left alone in her hut. Annie was so tired that she fell asleep straight away.

The night was beautiful at this point; everyone could hear the noises of the crickets. The lights of the stars were shining in the sky. Annie awoke and looked everywhere. She saw Alan lying down close to her. She gave him a cuddle.

"You can't sleep my Parrot, aren't you tired." said Annie.

"Annie, my little Annie! I have something to tell you." began Alan as he raised his head towards the little girl.

"Yes, Alan. I know that you have something to tell me. What is your secret? One day you are a Parrot and another, you are a powerful Golden Eagle. What is wrong?" asked Annie.

He wanted to answer but a mother Ibis whom shouted far off very aggressively stopped him.

"Oh, shut up! You don't have children to hush." The little ones started to shout causing the anger of their mother aciculate.

"You will tell me everything in the morning Alan. Sleep now." whispered Annie to Alan's ear.

Alan stuck against Annie's body and closed his eyes. He fell asleep in moments.

"Kui-kui-kui" "Kui-kui-kui" "Kui-kui-kui"

Annie heard close to her ears. She woke up and saw three chicks in her hut. She sat up and yawned. The chicks looked at her as she put a hand on her mouth.

"Excuse me if I yawned to loudly." said Annie.

"Kui-kui-kui "; "Kui-kui-kui "; "Kui-kui-kui" continued the chicks.

Annie smiled and took the three chicks in her arms. She gave them a cuddle.

"Where is your mother?" asked Annie.

"Mum went to look for food," answered one chick.

"Our mother is good to us, she gives us food and takes care of us," added the second chick.

"And where is your mother?" demanded the third chick.

"I don't have a mother. Peter the dad of Madge and Madeline said to me that I didn't have a mother," mumbled Annie sadly.

"Oh! ..." said one of the chicks in surprise.

"Every child has a mother," added the second.

"And why don't you have a mother?" Asked the third.

"My mum died at my birth and I don't have a dad either," replied Annie while gripping her fingers nervously.

"Oh, why is that?" asked one of the chicks while tilting her head.

Their mother entered Annie's hut; the female Western Capercaillie dropped the insect that she had within her beak and went in front of the little girl.

"Annie, my little Princess! These three monsters didn't spend hours bothering you, I hope." said the mother.

She walked around her babies and hugged them with her wings. She returned towards Annie.

"Annie, My name is Jane and these are my babies: Molly, Mimi and Natalie," continued the mother.

The female Western Capercaillie cut the flesh of the insect and gave it to the first, to the second then to the third chick.

"Mum, Princess Annie told us that she doesn't have a mother," said Molly

"Or a dad!" added Mimi.

"Oh, no!" exclaimed Jane.

"It's true mum!" continued Natalie.

"Her mum didn't feed her like you feed us. And her dad is surely like ours."

"Oh, your father always runs into other nests. It's not important for the birds to have a father. But for the humans, it is very important to have a mother and a father. Then my little Princess, where are your parents?" asked the mother Western Capercaillie.

Annie defended herself.

"I don't have a mother, I was born in a stable and my mother died at my birth. I was raised by Mrs Grandmother and Mister Grandfather."

The mother Western Capercaillie continued to feed her children. She stared at the little girl with a knowing glance. She came towards Annie and caressed her cheek with her right wing then went back again towards her chicks.

"Oh, poor you! Life is hard to live sometimes. You don't have a mum. Don't worry, I will be your mum if you want me to." said the mother to Annie while scraping the ground in search of food.

"Will you Mum? Will Annie be my little sister?" asked Mimi as she hopped.

"No, she will be the older sister because I am the little one," corrected Natalie.

"No, I am the older sister," shouted Molly.

Jane enlarged her wings and beat them violently; she hushed her children and made them stop arguing.

"Oh, oh, oh! We eat first and we discuss afterwards! Annie is also my daughter, Understood!" growled the mother. "If she doesn't have a dad, it is not a problem. Yours spends his time with other females. He's foolish like that."

A Hen left her nest and went into Annie's hut. She entered and spoke to Jane who pretended not hear her.

"Jane, I heard you. Don't speak anymore about Marc that way." clucked the female.

Jane went outside Annie's hut.

"Marc! Marc! Marc is not your husband," shouted Jane while walking round. "And don't talk to me like that in front of my children."

"Oh, why are you afraid they might hear something they shouldn't Jane. I just want to tell you not to speak about Marc that way, never again," continued the female

Jane went to bite her in the back and the female dodged the blow from her beak.

The female awkwardly ran away in fear to her nest and she awoke the male Western Capercaille that slept quietly.

"Marc, come and defend me," ordered the female.

"Marguerite, leave me alone. I am trying to sleep." refused Marc.

"Marc, Marc, Marc, you trust Marc. He likes all the females of the forest, which is why we are fifteen strong." screamed Jane while shaking herself like she were mad.

Marguerite came out then went back into her nest. She heard Jane shouting outside and as she followed her, she opened her beak.

"Oh, you're so jealous!" – growled Marguerite. "Jealous! Jealous!"

"I'm Jealous? I'm jealous! I'm jealous!!" Shouted Jane.

Jane scraped the ground while emitting a noise then she jumped on Marguerite and they started to fight. Annie left her hut and separated the two females.

"Oi, Hey, don't fight," shouted the little girl.

Marc, the male Western Capercaillie, left Marguerite's nest and flew around them. He flew at the height of Annie.

"Leave them to fight, my little Princess! To fight like they are mad. What they don't know is that I like them both." whispered the Western Capercaillie.

"Both? We are fifteen," growled Jane.

"We are three," spoke Marguerite.

"Jane, Marguerite, stop this fighting! I believe that I will go away if you want to fight, so go ahead," thundered Marc.

He went away followed by Marguerite. Annie turned to Jane and picked her up.

"Oh, my sweet mum! You don't need to fight. You know what, let's go for a walk. Why don't you show me around? I want to see the river Loisa," suggested Annie while carrying Jane away. Annie asked, "Alan, where is Alan?"

"He left very early this morning for the forest. I believe that he was sad," answered Mimi.

Alan the Parrot flew between the trees in the forest. He continued to fly without paying attention. He didn't see the tree in front of him and knocked his head.

"Ouch..." howled the bird.

A noise drew his attention, he raised his head and discovered Marty hung on the tree trunk.

"Hello Marty." started Alan.

"Hello Alan. What are you doing so close to my nest? Are you looking for the bag of gold coins?" asked the Jamaican Woodpecker.

"The bag of gold coins!" screamed Alan.

"Yes, the bag. My chicks found it in the forest." continued Marty

"Oh, I had already forgotten about that! Thank you very much Marty, this is the fortune of my Princess," added the Parrot. "Thank you very much!"

"Don't worry, we found it. Come, I will present my wife and my daughters to you." said the Woodpecker.

Alan followed Marty into the nest. He found a female Woodpecker with a red head and her chicks; Marty introduced his family by pointing to them with his wing.

"Alan, I introduce to you Lucy my wife. And here are my daughters: Leanne, Martine and Marcy."

"Hello Lucy and the girls!" greeted the Parrot.

"Kui-kui-kui" shouted the babies as a greeting.

"Your house is very nice!" said Alan to the female.

"Thank you." replied Lucy.

Marty went to the middle of the nest and added.

"In the days to come, you will be able to build a nest and to have a wife, children as well, why not!"

"No, no nest for me and no wife, nor babies." said Alan.

"Why not? You don't like our country? Graceland is green from the North to the South, from the West to the East. There is food everywhere. It is the ideal place to rest in spite of the birds of prey..." mumbled Marty as he saw Alan hopping nervously in the room.

"There is no place for Annie here. She must go to school and learn like all the little girls her age," explained the Parrot as he shook his head.

"Oh! You sound practically human. I don't need that for my children. A little food is enough for them," said Marty.

Alan and Marty were in full conversation when they heard a call for help.

"Help! Help, help!" howled a bird with a very powerful voice.

Alan and Marty left the nest. The Parrot wanted to follow the bird and the Woodpecker stopped his wing.

"Don't worry Alan; it is the horned screamer which shouts like that. It always does it to annoy other birds." reassured Marty.

"Annie, Annie." called Alan.

He flew away. He transformed himself into a Golden Eagle as the fear covered his body. Alan left at the speed of wind.

"Annie, Annie, where are you my little Annie?" continued the Golden Eagle, anxiously.

Alan flew higher between the trees and lost his way to the glade.

"Ah, ah ah ah!" "Ah, ah ah ah!" "Ah, ah ah ah!"

Alan believed he heard Annie's laughter far off. He rushed his landing to find Annie and Jane close to the river.

"Tom...!" exclaimed the Western Capercaillie.

Annie raised her eyes towards the sky. She watched Alan land and transform himself into a Parrot. She went towards him.

"No, it is not Tom but Alan my Parrot," said Annie to Jane.

"A Magic Parrot!

Oh, oh oh, we've seen everything now," continued Jane.

Annie took Alan in her arms.

"Alan, I looked for you everywhere this morning. I woke up and you weren't in the hut," said the little girl.

Alan touched the face of Annie with his wing. She looked at him with a glance full of fear and happiness.

"I didn't stop thinking about..." started the Parrot.

"About what you were going to tell me," cut Annie. "Alan, don't you worry. I will like you no matter what form you take."

"Even when I become a vulture?" asked the Parrot seriously.

"What is this about you being a Vulture Mister my Parrot?" growled Annie disbelievingly.

"I am a magic bird which does all these things," explained Alan at the same time as swivelling on one leg.

He fell on the ground and pretended to die. Annie came close to him then opened his beak to see if he was still breathing. After having noticed that he was alive, she gave him a small slap on the beak then a kiss on the head.

"Like how did you clean the house in the blink of an eye or become a Parrot which transforms himself into a powerful Golden Eagle. Do you know how you do it?" added Annie.

"I don't know how I manage to do it. I know that as soon as I feel you are in danger, I become aggressive and transform myself into a Golden Eagle. I become a Parrot again when all is calm," confessed Alan.

Annie took him in her arms and gave him a cuddle. She said to him sadly, as they walked.

"A faithful friend, who will never leave me?" Asked Annie.

"Yes my little Annie, I will never leave you..." answered Alan at the same time rolling his eyes.

She started laughing. They suddenly heard a noise between the trees. Annie went in search of Jane and saw her in the sky.

"Marc, come here! Where are you going?" shouted Jane.

The Western Capercaillie was following her husband, the other female Jane was flying behind Marc.

"Mum, mum, come back here," ordered Annie.

"Oh, Alan! My mother is going to fight again. And if Marc could only have one female this wouldn't happen."

Annie gave him a kiss on the beak. Alan raised his head towards the little girl and opened his wings. He looked intensely at Annie.

"Annie! My little Annie, I am your grandfather!" said the Parrot, seriously.

Annie stopped a moment and looked at him, quite confused. She dropped down abruptly then she asked again.

"My Grandfather? Mister Grandfather?"

"Yes." answered Alan.

"My grandfather has disappeared and nobody knows where he has gone. He was so old and he had a wheelchair," added Annie as she got to her feet.

Alan stood in front of her; he started to beat his wings nervously.

"I am Mis-ter yo-ur grand-father!" stammered the Parrot.

"Do not talk in long fancy words! I forbid you to do so.

Mister Grandfather was a man and you're a bird," continued Annie.

"No. I am human. It is Marvel the witch who transformed me into this." explained Alan.

Annie opened her eyes and sat down again. She pointed a threatening finger at him.

"Marvel, the female Parrot that you were going to marry. A witch!" exclaimed the little girl.

Alan opened his wings and shook them a little. He went in front of Annie and sat down on her legs.

"And why do you think I refused to marry her?" asked the Parrot.

"Alan, why would Marvel have transformed you into a bird? You said to me that she wasn't your type of bird," added Annie.

"She transformed me because I wanted to help you. I went to her house asking for help," answered the bird. "I wanted her to find someone of your mother's family and also to tell her that Kirsty has to stop miss-treating you.

And then, she transformed me into a Parrot. She told me that I will live the life of a Parrot, a life of an Eagle also a Vulture, and then I will belong to her forever."

The little girl picked him up. She gave him a cuddle, but did not understand anything of what he was saying.

"Alan, I don't know what this means," stated Annie.

"Me either, I don't know. I really don't know," answered Alan.

"Oh what a mess this is. Why did you do it?" asked Annie as she wiped the tears from her eyes.

"I couldn't bear to see you suffer anymore," cried Alan.

"Oh, grandfather! You didn't have to sacrifice yourself for me!" Screamed Annie.

"I didn't sacrifice myself. She just transformed me into a Parrot." admitted Alan

She interrupted him by closing his beak with her two fingers. Alan saw a tear running on her cheek.

"We will go back to England and we will find this Marvel. And you will become a man again. I loved you more as you were and when I was pushing your wheelchair."

"My little Annie! What have I done?"

She hugged Alan to make him feel better then they looked at the Pelicans, Ducks, the Swans and their children playing in the water, which made them both, smile again.

"Could you bring some fish to the glade, please?" asked Annie to the Pelicans.

A big White Pelican leapt into the air, its neck inflated with water and fish. Another followed him then introduced himself to Annie.

"I am Guy and this is Roger, jump on my back. We're going back to the Central Glade."

Annie jumped on his back and they flew away towards the glade. When they arrived, Guy put Annie down and she looked at Roger vomiting the water and fish from his beak, which had narrowed. Roger said to the birds close to Annie's hut.

"Go to the forest and try to find some wood! Annie will make a barbecue," ordered the Brown Pelican.

The birds left to look for wood at the same time as making a great noise while they beat their wings. They returned each one of them with wood fixed to their claws. Annie took the fish and cleaned them in the mouth of another Pelican who ate the rest. The little girl managed to make a fire by using two stones and Alan emitted a noise of joy as he flapped his wings strongly.
"Oh, you're doing very well. We will eat fish today," said Alan to his grandaughter.
Annie put the fish one by one on a stick and positioned it close to the fire. She sat down at the side while looking at them cooking. She took Alan in her arms and cradled his feathery body without saying a word. The little girl took some fish then gave them to her grandfather as well as to the birds that were close to her.
"Thank you big sister!" mumbled Molly, Mimi and Natalie through their food.

Chapter 4 - The return.

Annie left the water, she wore her dress and looked at herself. She went towards Alan who was resting near the river.

"Alan, what are we doing now?" asked Annie.

"We are going back home," answered Alan as he stood up.

He opened his wings fully and transformed himself into an Eagle. He went to the edge of the river, drank some water and came back towards Annie while beating his wings. "Jump on my back, we're leaving."

"Grandad, first I must say goodbye to my Mum, Jane." added the girl.

Annie jumped on his back and Alan flew away towards the glade where they found Jane fighting with a female Grouse.

"Mum, stop fighting! Stop fighting now." shouted Annie from the sky.

Alan landed and the little girl got off his back. She went to separate the two birds. She tore Jane off and gave her a kiss on the beak. The female Grouse fled.

"Mum! You shouldn't fight anymore. Promise me before I leave!" scolded Annie.

"Leave! Where are you going? I will twist the neck of that, which takes you from me..."Screamed Jane.

"You will twist nobody's neck," said Annie firmly. "I came to say goodbye. I am going back to England. Where are my sisters?"

She heard cries coming from her hut. She entered and found the chicks sitting on the large leaf that used to be Annie's bed.

"Kui-kui-kui." they shouted.

"Hello Annie, we're where you left us." said Mimi.

"Where are you going?" asked Nathalie.

"I'm going home. I am going with my Magic Parrot to England." answered Annie who was approaching them.

"Is he really a Magic Parrot?" asked Molly

"Is it true? Is Alan a Magic Parrot?" added Mimi.

"What can he do for me? I would like to leave this forest too." said Nathalie.

Their mother Jane approached her babies and scratched her beak on the ground to threaten them and they ran to hide in the hut.

"You are going nowhere!" thundered the mother.

"Mum, it is Nathalie who wants to go away. Not Molly and me." complained Mimi.

"Mum when I grow up, I will go away." said Nathalie, seriously.

Jane ignored this comment she took a dead insect, she cut it in one, two then three pieces and she put each one of them into the beak of her chicks. She went towards Annie and wrapped her in her wings.

"My little daughter, I will really miss you. Why are you leaving us?" asked Jane

"My beloved Mum! I must go! I must help my Grandad." answered Annie who was kneeling in front of Jane.

The female Western Capercaillie turned the little girl around who sat down sadly.

"Anything I can do? Oh, come here! You break my heart." continued the mother.

Jane opened her wings, she took Annie's face between her two wings and they kissed each other. Molly, Mimi and Nathalie joined them. Already, Alan was longing to get back to England. He looked at Annie.

"My little Princess, we have to go." said Alan, impatiently.

Annie left the family while waving goodbye and she jumped on Alan's back and he flew away. Annie was comfortably sitting on the Eagle's back when she saw a black cloud, on her right, approaching them.

"Alan, It's Bill and the others!" shouted Annie.

Alan looked on his right and saw a crowd of birds following them. Marty parted from the crowd with a package fixed to his beak. He came to sit down on the Eagle's back and Annie caught the small bag.

"My Princess, you were going without your gold coins." said Marty.

"My gold coins?" Wondered Annie.

"The gold coins that Madam Carla left you for your inheritance," explained Alan. "The bag that Kirsty was angry about."

"Did My Grandmother leave me a fortune?" asked the little girl in surprise.

"Oh, yes!" replied Alan.

Annie turned to Marty and thanked him.

"Thank you my friend. Now, we must seek the road to England."

"I can show you the way to England if you want me to," proposed Marty.

"I must say that I come from Jamaica and all Jamaican Woodpeckers know England. First of all, we must take care of this crowd."

The birds approached and formed a circle all around them. Bill flew towards the Eagle. He violently beat his wings in the air.

"You wanted to leave us without saying goodbye?" began the Shoebill stork.

Alan then also violently flapped his wings and confronted him. Bill lowered his eyes.

"I go when and where it pleases Me." thundered Alan.

"I didn't forbid you to leave but there is nobody to replace you as king." said Bill.

"Bill, I am not your king. You know it well enough, you can take the throne. You managed very well last time, as a king." stated Alan.

"You were good to us. You defeated Mortal and we couldn't let you go without saying thanks and goodbye. And to the Princess too." continued Bill.

Annie while watching them speak, intervened.

She addressed herself to Bill.

"Bill, don't worry. We will surely return one day. I didn't have time to fix your crown. Give it to me."

Annie removed the crown from the head of the large bird. She folded the long feather into two and took another; she made a beautiful crown in such a short space of time. When she had finished, she put it back on Bill's head.

"Now, birds of Graceland, this is your king." screamed Alan.

"With a beautiful crown on his head. Voila!" added Annie.

Bill beat his wings and turned towards the crowd. He exclaimed happily.

"I am now the king for real!"

"Yippy hurrah. Yippy hurrah! Long live our king!" sang the crowd of birds.

Alan beat his wings violently and imposed a silence in the air. He flew and went above all the birds.

"I don't leave you now. So I do not say farewell, I say goodbye. If you want to see me, think strongly and I will be there with you." said Alan proudly.

"Yippy Hurrah." sang the crowd.

A black male Swan stepped aside from crowd and went towards Alan. He showed the birds with his wing.

"You cannot go without seeing our parade." begged the black swan.

"Which parade?" asked Annie.

"The parade of goodbye for our beautiful Princess." answered Bill.

The birds placed themselves in row by size and weight followed by the birds of paradise. They started making rotations on the left, on the right while performing grand aerobatics. Some drew away while singing in the sky the sentence - We love you Annie Princess - and the others - We hope to see you again soon -.

Alan beat his wings and left. Annie waved goodbye to them with both her hands. Alan and Marty went quickly through the wind, they thought they heard a voice far off.

"Wait! Wait!" screamed the voice.

They turned around and they saw Jane, the female Western Capercaillie, rejoining them.

"Wait for me! Wait for me, please!" shouted Jane.

They stopped and watched her beating painfully her wings because her species cannot fly that fast. Jane rejoined them, breathlessly.

"Annie my daughter, I could not let you leave without giving you the news. Marc has returned to me. He swore to me that he will not leave us again and that he will always love me." said Jane to Annie.

The little girl took her in her arms. She gave her a cuddle.

"Oh, my beloved Mum! I am happy for you. Tell dad, I will come back one day. Give a kiss to my sisters: Molly, Mimi and Nathalie. I will miss you all," said Annie laughing.

"I will tell them! Goodbye and see you soon darling. I wish you all the best." continued Jane.
She kissed Annie and flew away. Alan, Marty and Annie looked at her flying back and they continued on their way.

The birds were flying for what seemed like hours. It was almost dawn when they saw the first glimpses of the day, Marty accelerated his descent followed by Alan.
"England, here we are. Buckingham Palace is surely not far from here. I see the London bridge... "shouted Marty while stopping abruptly.
Alan got annoyed.
"No, no... We lost our way. We are not going to London but to Manchester Marty."
"Manchester is about three hours towards the North West. Let's go!" confirmed the Woodpecker by shaking his head.
They headed towards the north. A strong gale shook them. The birds extended their wings to rebalance themselves.
"Annie, how are you doing?" asked Alan as Annie gave him a kiss on the head.
"Fine! Go ahead my powerful Eagle." answered Annie.
Alan plunged into the wind. They flew hours upon hours above the clouds.
The birds fought against the gale. They descended a few miles under the clouds and continued quietly.

"You don't have to worry. We're going forwards." reassured Marty.

"The rain! We're home!" screamed Alan, happily. "Annie, darling! Don't you smell the ground below us?"

The little girl breathed deeply and gave him a slap on the shoulder as she shouted proudly.

"Grandad, we are home!"

Marty swivelled in the air as he made some aerobatics. He stopped on their level, with his wings covering his chest.

"Yippy... we're here!" screamed Marty with a voice full of joy.

The Jamaican Woodpecker lengthened his legs and opened his wings widely Annie looked below the wings of the Eagle and proudly, She heard Marty announcing.

"Ladies and Gentleman, here is Manchester!"

Annie opened her arms as a sign of victory and started to shout. She watched Marty twisting and turning in the sky, under the rain.

"Yippy, yippy! Manchester... I am home." Screamed Annie.

"Hurrah. Hurrah." shouted Marty.

"Let's go towards Hyde Road, we have to find Ardwick Green Park to know if we really have arrived." said Alan to Marty as he plunged towards the ground.

It was dawn as they went down to land, as they were reaching the ground; Alan had a hunch of danger. He was suddenly scared for Annie. He stopped and looked at Marty strangely.

"Marty, I feel danger. Can you stay behind while I go to see what is happening?" proposed Alan.

"Shall I call for Help?" asked the Woodpecker. "I need to find a tree to call the others."

"We don't need help. I feel danger but I cannot judge where from. I have to land or transform myself into a Parrot to know. But I can't do it with Annie on my back." explained Alan.

Marty went on the level of the Eagle and tried to understand. He shook his head strongly.

"What do I have to do?" asked the Woodpecker.

"Stay behind. You should land only when we are out of danger. You must especially keep the bag of gold coins with you. If we are caught, you should return to Graceland and keep the gold coins," he continued while lowering his head. "One day, you will bring them to my Grandaughter when she is a grown up."

A tear ran out of his eyes. Annie saw the tear and tapped him on the neck. She gently gave him a kiss on the head.

"Grandad, nothing will happen to us!" Annie reassured him.

"I'm going to see first." said Marty to comfort him.

"No, don't go there. I feel something more serious..." predicted Alan.

"You feel danger. Is it Marvel?" asked Annie.

Alan shook his head positively. He looked at Marty strangely.

"What I want is to protect Annie's future. Keep the bag of gold coins with you at all times. It is an order!"

"And why's that?" asked the Woodpecker while refusing to obey.

"Marty don't argue with me. Do as I say." thundered Alan with a voice mixed with fear and uncertainty.

Marty flew on the same level as Annie and She gave him the small bag of gold coins. He took it in his beak and went in a different direction.

Alan followed his course and he went down lower. He flew miles and miles and he went to land above a large building. His glance traversed the city centre and he took to the air again.

Alan perched on 111 Piccadilly and he dropped Annie from his back.

"Take a rest Annie, we are close to the home now." suggested Alan.

Annie walked around on the top of the building and returned close to him. Alan looked at the cars passing on London Road. They stayed there a few minutes and Alan made a sign to Annie with his head.

The little girl went up on his back again and they set off again; Alan saw the park, which extended gracefully and read the sign "Ardwick Green Park."

Alan landed on the entry of the park and Annie went down from his back. He felt some presence on the trees, like white shades.

He beckoned to Annie to bend down and he whispered to her ears.

"Annie, I feel some presence on the trees, like invisible birds. At the end of the park, there is an alley, which leads to Marvel's house. Go ahead, I will cover you! As soon as the way is free, I will join you there." whispered Alan.

Alan went in the middle of the park, raised his head and saw passers by. He got scared and he wanted to fly away. He heard a voice, which he recognised straight away. "Marvel!" shouted Alan.

"An Eagle! An Eagle in the park!" howled the old woman.

Marvel went towards him and extended her hands, trying to catch him. Alan defended himself. A mysterious force prevented Alan from flying and nailed him down. He wanted to fly away, He opened his wings to dash, but Marvel blocked him by concentrating her powers on him. "What do you think you are doing?" asked the witch. "I want you to die!" Annie looked at the scene without understanding what was happening, Marvel continued to howl aloud, waking the neighbourhood.

"I'm being attacked. Help! Help... "Screamed the old woman.

She alerted the neighbours and the soldiers from King's Company left their bunks to circle on every side of Alan. Annie had time to react, she saw one man moving toward the middle of the park with a rifle to hand. He aimed and shot, it hit Alan on the shoulder.

Annie could not stand for this man shooting Alan.

The little girl left her hiding-place and went to take the rifle off the hands of the man.

"Don't kill him. Don't kill him. Alan... Alan!" cried Annie.

"My shoulder..." said Alan as he collapsed.

The Golden Eagle fell to the ground. He saw Marvel smiling. He closed his eyes and felt like he had no control of his body anymore, but he heard Annie screaming and a woman saying.

"Annie. It is Annie, the little orphan who had disappeared, carried by an Eagle." "Annie of the Granger family?" asked another woman.

"Kirsty, here is the little orphan who lived at your home." added a third woman. Alan heard the noise of a slap and Annie howled with pain. She struggled wildly in Kirsty hands.

"Oh, I though I got rid of you!" howled Kirsty while holding her firmly.

Alan heard this voice in his head again and again. He did not feel anything anymore as he passed out.

Annie was wearing a long tight yellow dress. She had her long black hair combed and attached in a chignon. She had swollen eyes, a sign she had cried too much. She was not only saddened because of the punishment, which she had received from Kirsty, but also because of what had happened to Alan.

"Grandad..." Cried Annie.

She remembered him falling and standing up again. She saw his wing covered in blood. Annie started to cry again and again. She wiped her eyes with her hand.

Peter held Annie's suitcase in one hand and on the other, he held her hand tightly against his. They arrived in front of a large building and Annie read the sign on the orphanage's gate 'Little angels.' She shivered.

They went in front of the large door. Peter, without a word, tightened the small fingers of Annie against his once more and pressed the buzzer. A big woman opened the door.

"We have an appointment with Mrs Deborah Crane." said Peter as he gave her a note.

The woman stepped aside to let them in. They followed her in a dark corridor. Annie looked on her left and on her right. She looked at the walls covered in strange and sinister paintings. She was not scared by the sight, but she whimpered and attracted the attention of the woman. They arrived in front of the stairs.

"Take the stairs and follow the alley on your left and Mrs Crane's office is on the right." pointed the woman.

"Thank you." said Peter without smiling.

The office of Mrs Crane was roomy, the walls were painted in blue and the only source of light was coming from a large open window. Annie was attracted to a vase filled with yellow and blue flowers. They reminded her of to the colour of Alan, her Parrot. She approached the vase and touched the flowers. She started moaning. On their right, they saw another door. Peter went towards Annie and pulled her by the hand.

He made her sit on a bench. He knocked on the door. An old woman opened it.

"Mr Granger, I've been waiting for you!" said the woman.

Peter beckoned with his finger towards Annie so she would follow him. She stood up and went towards them. They entered and discovered a room that had walls covered with sinister paintings like in the corridor. In the middle, close to a table, stood another woman whose face was covered in wrinkles.

Annie judged the expression of the old woman. She was rigid, she was commanding. The little girl pouted. She lowered her head, she inflated her cheeks and she pouted again. She did not stop pulling this look.

"Mrs Katie Pickles, the housekeeper." introduced the headmistress.

The housekeeper bent towards Annie and she looked at her without a smile. "Annie... Correct?" asked the housekeeper.

Annie crossed her arms on her chest and looked at the woman without smiling. "Yes Madam..." answered Annie.

"Yes Mrs Pickles." indicated the housekeeper as she put a finger on Annie's nose.

Mrs Crane looked at the scene then turned towards Peter, she showed him a chair.

"Please take a seat, Mr Granger." said the headmistress.

She showed Annie a bench in a corner of the room and asked her to go there. The little girl went to sit down on the bench. The headmistress continued addressing Peter.

"So Annie Carla Benedicta Granger never went to school. And why is this?"

"Annie never showed the will to study or go to school," lied Peter as he cleared his throat.

"She is stubborn and does not like to work. She is always lazy,"

"That is not the point, you should have sent her to school" intervened the headmistress.

"I tried but she always skipped classes and she didn't obey my simple orders." continued Peter.

"And I'm telling you that is not the point. Every child should go to school, that is," growled Mrs Crane. "You should have sent your child to school."

"She is not my child, she is an orphan born in the stable of my property and I did a lot by giving her a roof. Now, I can't keep her anymore because I don't have anymore space in my house. My wife Kirsty is expecting another child as well."

Mrs Crane looked seriously at Annie who was balancing on her feet, she had lowered her face.

"How old is she?" asked Mrs Crane.

"She is eight years old." answered Peter.

"You said that she is an orphan? And why has she got your name then?" continued the headmistress.

"I didn't have any other name to give her. Her mother died at her birth. I couldn't find her family and I got stuck with her," added Peter.

"Don't worry. I will pay you to take her... "

Peter was embarrassed by the flood of questions and unceasingly remembered the words of his wife. She didn't want Annie to return in her house.

The headmistress put her two hands on the table and said.

"I agree we shall take Annie here," she continued while making a pause. "We have a school, dormitories, a refectory, a library. The orphanage is a little like a boarding school. We will see what we can do to catch her up with the rest of the students. For the moment, I will put her with children her own age I will see what level she is on, but don't worry she'll be able to catch up."

"Thank you very much, Mrs Crane!" mumbled Peter.

He stood up and they shook hands without smiling. Peter looked at Annie. He took a handkerchief from his pocket and he wiped his face.

Mrs Crane beckoned to the housekeeper to approach.

"Mrs Pickles, Could you take Annie to the girl's dormitory?" asked the headmistress.

The housekeeper took Annie by the hand. The little girl followed her without stumbling.

They walked through many corridors and Annie believed that they would never end.

Finally, Annie saw a door. Mrs Pickles opened it and they entered. "Claire. Where are you Claire?" called the housekeeper.

A little girl with short black hair, roughly the same size of Annie came and bent her knee. "Did you call me Madam?" asked Claire.

"Yes, Claire! Come here, please." continued Mrs Pickles.

The housekeeper stepped aside to let Annie pass. She saw ten well arranged beds. Mrs Pickles showed Annie to Claire.

"I introduce to you Annie Carla Benedicta Granger. Make her a place in your room." added the woman.

They heard a voice from behind the curtains. A little girl with blonde hair came towards them and she took the hand of the housekeeper.

"Mother, does she not have a family!" said the little girl.

Mrs Pickles gave her a kiss on her cheeks and went towards the curtains to discover two other girls who were smiling. The woman went back towards the girl with blond hair.

"Joanne! What were you doing behind the curtains? Where are the others?" asked Mrs Pickles.

"We were playing hide-and-seek. And for the others..." answered Joanne.

She tightened her lips as she looked at Annie and pointed a finger under the beds on her right and her left. Mrs Katie Pickles struck the hands and small bodies crawled from under the beds.

"It is time for your nap. Go to the bed!" thundered Mrs Pickles.

They jumped without stumbling on the beds and the housekeeper looked at Annie.

"Annie, take the empty bed at the bottom," continued Mrs Pickles as she watched Annie move towards the bed and lie down without a word. The housekeeper went and put her suitcase on a small table close to the bed. She looked around carefully.

"We will meet again in the refectory for dinner, at seven o'clock."

On this, she left after taking care to switch off the light and closed the door well behind her.

Alan the Eagle woke up. He felt an atrocious pain in his right wing. He could not move and he felt a chain on his leg.

He opened his eyes and saw that he was in a large cage. He inspected his body and he saw an iron chain to his left leg and a bandage on his wing.

The Eagle tried to unchain himself with the help of his beak, but he could not. He gave one blow, two then three. Nothing, he remained immobilised. Alan was discouraged and sat down. He looked at the room and saw a small window where the sunlight entered.

"Where am I? Annie, where are you? My little Annie!" cried Alan. He stood up and tried to move. "How did I come here?" He closed his eyes and relived the scene of the park, he continued. "Oh, my God! Does Annie believe that I am dead? I have to leave."

Alan wanted to open his wings and he felt so bad that he howled in pain. He sat down again immediately.

"Ouch! What hurts so much!" shouted Alan.

He turned his head towards his wing and with his beak, tried to take off the bandage. With a powerful stroke, he detached the knot. He beat the left wing with the aim of unrolling the bandage, which involved a noise of beating his wing. A male nurse opened the door and entered in the room. He carried a white blouse and looked at Alan trying to undo his dressing.

The male nurse put a hand in the cage and tried to remake the dressing. Alan bit him and the young man ran outside the room shouting. Alan did not have the time to get rid of the bandage when a troop of male nurses entered the room.

They encircled the cage and without understanding what was happening Alan received an injection, which made him sleepy.

His head started to whirl and he looked at them, powerlessly as they remade his dressing.

As soon as they finished, they left, leaving him under the effects of the product. Alan remained lying down during the following hours. He tried to concentrate on finding Annie by the force of his thoughts.

"Annie, Annie where are you?" said Alan to himself unconsciously.

He directed all his attention towards his Grandaughter and a light crossed his spirit. Alan received a flash and he shook himself. He saw Annie sitting alone in a corner. The children were playing everywhere.

"One would say a school playground. A school! Annie in a school?" said Alan. Alan opened his eyes and shook his head. He was not dreaming. He believed he saw his Grandaughter in a school playground.

"I don't dream. Is this the effect of the injection?" wondered the Eagle.

He closed his eyes again and redirected his thoughts towards Annie.

"Annie, Annie where are you? thought Alan strongly.

He was peering at the vision as they continued. He saw a little blonde girl coming towards Annie and giving her a slap on the head. Annie fled, she went to hide behind a wall and she started to cry.

Suddenly an anger mixed with pain seized Alan. He tried to release himself from the chains but he could not move. He concentrated again and saw the little girl going towards Annie and giving her another slap on the head.

A boy came close to separate them. He pointed at the little girl with his finger and she fled. The Bell vibrated and all the children went into a row in front of a woman. They entered the classrooms silently and Annie sat down close to the boy.

The teacher was in front of the board and was teaching. She noticed that one of the pupils was making a noise at the bottom of the classroom.

She went behind him, then removed him from his chair and sent him to the front of the classroom. Alan could not understand what was being said. His vision was not very clear as the effect of the product had not disappeared.

"It's real, it's not the effect of the product." he said to himself while remembering the word of Marvel (- you will live the life of a Parrot, of an Eagle and of a Vulture and you will belong to me-). The witch pointed her magic wand, he heard a noise and was transformed into a Parrot. "Magic Capacity!" continued Alan.

He could transform himself from time to time into a Parrot, then into an Eagle. And if he had more magic capacities he did not know how to use them yet.

"I can't believe it! I have magic powers."

Previously, He did not know very well how to change his appearance because he was more or less pushed by anger or the desire to help his Grandaughter.

To concentrate, that is! He had to concentrate for better knowing himself. For the moment, He enjoyed looking at Annie in her classroom. However if he could understand what was said it would make things easier and maybe he would hear where she was. Alan concentrated a bit harder he asked himself.

"Annie, what are you saying?"

Alan suddenly heard the teacher speaking.

"Today's lesson is based on the human body and its principal parts," she looked at the pupils while going between the chairs and spoke to a quiet classroom. "I want a volunteer who wants to be a human sample?" Nobody answered. The teacher went in front of all her pupils. "Nobody wants to come forwards, then I will choose." she said while designating a pupil with her finger "You over there, Paul."

A little boy stood up and went to the front of the class. The teacher went beside him and asked.

"What do you think, how many parts does the human body have? Look closely at your classmate Paul."

Nobody answered. The teacher peered around the room, she looked at her pupils in turn. Annie raised her hand.

"Annie!" said the teacher.

"The human body has three parts." answered the little girl softly after having stood up.
"Well done. Five points for Annie." exclaimed the mistress.
Alan smiled and he said.
"That's my girl."
With opened eyes he remembered his first miracle. Alan the Parrot flying in the house and cleaning all under the amused and surprised eye of Annie. He saw his Grandaughter following him everywhere in the house while shouting, happily. For the first time, he had given her happiness. She had been reading the pages of the books in hiding-places, because she was not allowed to go to school.
A good education and a good school that is all he dreamed of for his Grandaughter. He closed his eyes once more and fell asleep in peace.

Chapter 5 the visit.

Katie Pickles entered boldly into the girl's dormitory to find Annie and Joanne fighting. Joanne had succeeded in throwing Annie to the ground.

"Another little girl without a family." exclaimed Joanne as she struck Annie.

The other children were laughing and shouting. The housekeeper took a whistle from the pocket of her dress and blew into it. Everyone stopped. She went towards them and seized Annie by the shoulder.

"What are you doing?" asked the enraged woman.

The little girl tried to release herself from the housekeeper's hands but the woman held her firmly. She put her nails and scratched Annie knowingly.

"Mrs Pickles, it is not me who started this. It is..." answered Annie while crying. Without leaving her the time to continue, she inserted her nails in the flesh of Annie. The girls laughed.

"You took something which didn't belong to you?" shouted the housekeeper.

Annie wanted to answer and Mrs Pickles shushed her with a finger. Joanne put her two hands on her hips and started smiling. She did not stop; she looked at Annie and made a grimace. Annie restrained herself from screaming.

The housekeeper dragged her by the shoulder and opened a little door in the dormitory. She threw Annie in a small cell.

"No food for you today." she added. She turned towards the other girls, she wiped the face of her daughter Joanne and told the girls. "Everyone to the refectory."

Mrs Pickles pushed them towards the door and they left.

Annie crossed her feet. She was not crying anymore when she heard voices calling her. She approached the door and heard two people looking her.

"Annie, where are you?" they asked. "Where are you Annie?"

She distinguished the voices of Gavin and Claire. She knocked strongly on the door of the cell.

"I am here! I am in the cell." shouted Annie.

"I knew that Mrs Pickles would put you in this cursed cell. But I kept it to myself," claimed Claire.

"Gavin, the keys!" Claire asked.

Gavin took the keys from his pocket and gave them to Claire who opened the door. She helped Annie to leave the cell. Annie wiped the dust from her dress and shook hands with Gavin.

"Were you punished because of Joanne?" asked Claire.

She nodded and showed them the marks left by the housekeeper.

"Come, we brought you something to eat." said Claire.

Gavin took a package and gave it to Annie who opened it. She sat down and started to eat. The boy touched Annie's hair to reassure her.

"No need to be scared of Joanne. She threatens you because you're new at the orphanage, she does it with everyone."

"Don't worry, I will teach her a lesson tonight when she comes to bed," promised Claire while kneeling close to her.

Gavin looked at Claire and smiled. The girl gave him a slap on the shoulder. They began to laugh.

"Annie you need to learn how to defend yourself," said the boy. "Or just tell the headmistress about the bullying."

He stood up and made some movements miming karate chops the girls laughed at him. They heard steps coming from the corridor and they calmed down.

"Shush... Let's go!" continued Gavin.

He opened the door and beckoned to the girls to follow him. The children travelled endless corridors leading to a door. They opened it and they were on a porch. Claire opened her arms largely and said.

"My favourite place in the entire world!"

Gavin took Annie by the hand and led her to the middle of the terrace porch.

"Here is our paradise. The only place where one can reach the sky, where one feels really free," exclaimed the boy.

Gavin went in a corner and picked two flowers in a vase. He gave them to Claire and Annie.

Claire felt the flower and looked at Annie. She beckoned to her asking her to do the same. Annie put the flower in front of her nose and tickled her nose.

"Atchoo..." Sneezed Annie.

She shook her head. Claire and Gavin laughed at her. Annie went to sit down at the edge of the large porch and looked at the sky as she began to cry.

"Oh, my Parrot! My Grandad Eagle!"

A tear ran out of her eye, she wiped her face with her hand. Claire approached her and took her hand.

"You miss your Grandfather don't you?" said Claire.

Annie agreed by nodding her head. Gavin smiled then he put his hand through his hair.

"Don't worry. By the grace of fate, you will see him again Annie, I hope to have a family which will like me for me." continued Claire.

"Lets go back, the refectory will be empty and everyone will be in bed.

We won't be seen on our way back." said Gavin while coming towards them.

The girls stood up and they went away quickly. Claire held Annie by the hand and squeezed it. They followed Gavin who was leading the way.

"The way is free, lets go!" said Gavin to the girls. They entered the girl's dormitory and Annie entered the cell. Claire and Gavin hid under the beds. The door sprung open, Mrs Pickles entered and went to get Annie from the cell.

"Mrs Crane would like to see you," said the housekeeper as she held Annie firmly. She added while leaving "I hope you've learnt your lesson." Claire and Gavin left the beds. They followed Annie and the housekeeper to the headmistress' office and listened at the door. They heard Joanne explaining herself and she pointed her finger at Annie.

"Headmistress, Annie was the first to hit me." lied Joanne.

"Annie Carla, what do you say about that? The fight between classmates is strictly prohibited in this orphanage." growled Mrs Crane as she looked at the little girl wiping the tears with the hand.

"Headmistress, Annie is a naughty girl. She can't behave well and fights for anything," lied Mrs Pickles as she defended her daughter. "She asks for things and when one refuses her, she harms herself like those marks she has on her wrists."

Mrs Crane took Annie by the hands and pointed at her wrists. She shook her head after noticing the wounds were not healing. She went to take the first aid box and made bandages for Annie.

"Mrs Pickles, you can leave." continued the headmistress.

The housekeeper left followed by her daughter. Mrs Crane went to sit down and pointed a finger at a chair to Annie that the little girl sat down without a word. Annie looked at Mrs Crane looking through her files without saying anything. She tired and put the files on the desk.

"Annie, do you know why you are here?" asked the old woman.

"No, headmistress." Answered Annie.

"You are here simply because you are to be punished. Everyday during one week, you will come to stay here with me after class. You will take your meal with me, understood!" said the headmistress.

"Yes, Headmistress." replied Annie raising the head.

Claire was jumping across the tables in the classroom with two others girls. She stopped when she heard some laughter coming from a group of girls. She jumped from the table where she joined the group of girls, who began to surround Annie. She made her way through them.

"What's so funny?" asked Claire.

"Annie has sisters who are birds called Molly, Mimi and Nathalie," said a little girl.

"And her mother is called Jane, a female Western Capercaillie." added another girl.

The children laughed at Annie who got angry and she said seriously.

"I am telling the truth and my dad Marc has three partners."

Joanne slapped Annie on the head. She tried to defend herself but Joanne continued.

"What a silly girl! A little girl who thinks birds are her parents. What a pity!" mocked Joanne.

Claire intervened; she applied a good slap to Joanne and looked down at her. She grabbed her ears.

"It's better than a little girl who has a father who never comes to see her." shouted Claire as she let Joanne go.

Joanne started to cry and pushed Annie who fell. Claire put herself in front of her to protect Annie.

"Annie, stand up and push her back," ordered Claire.

"Fight! Fight! Fight! Fight!" Shouted the children.

Annie refused to push Joanne and another boy pushed Annie with his foot. Gavin punched the boy and the boy shouted. The children did not see Diane Parker in front of the door. The teacher coughed and they calmed down. Each one of them regained their seats.

The headmistress entered the classroom and stood in front of the pupils. Diane smiled.

"Today, we are going to have a special lesson. The headmistress, Mrs Crane will be with us throughout the lesson which will be based on a flying species, of bird." stated the teacher.

The headmistress went to stand at the bottom of the classroom and her attention went on Annie who was not focused at all. She was thinking about her Grandfather and what had become of him.

"Mister my Grandfather, I need you. I don't want to stay in this orphanage any more.

I've already spent to much time without you. Come find me." cried Annie suddenly.

Alan opened his eyes suddenly. He believed he was hearing his Grandaughter calling him. While he was asleep, was it a dream? He stood up and shook himself. He felt the pain in his wing again. He looked at his chained leg. He looked into his cage and saw some meat on a plate.
"Bleurk... raw flesh!" shouted the Eagle.
He drank water in a bowl, which was close to the plate in the cage. He stood up and shook his head. Alan heard Annie speaking to him while groaning in the vision. He sat on his legs and closed his eyes.
"My powerful Eagle come find me and take me far from here on your wings." cried Annie.
Alan heard the class's laughter; he stood up again, sat again and closed his eyes. He directed his attention toward Annie and he was pulled by the vision.
Diane Parker went towards Annie.
"Annie, what have you just said?" asked the teacher.
"Mister my powerful Eagle, come find me and take me far from here on your wings." repeated Annie.
The pupils laughed at her even more. The teacher launched a glance towards the headmistress.
"Annie, who is Mister your powerful Eagle?" asked Diane.

"My Grandad!" answered Annie without looking at her.

"Is your Grandfather an Eagle?" continued the teacher.

"Yes," answered Annie who was pouting stubbornly.

"And where is he?" asked Diane Parker.

"I don't know Madam the teacher." answered Annie.

"Diane, call me Diane. Talk to me, tell me about Molly, Mimi and Nathalie." asked Diane.

Annie brightened herself and smiled. She cleared her throat.

"Molly, Mimi and Nathalie are my sisters. Our dad is called Marc and our Mum is Jane. She is always fighting with other females of Graceland." told Annie.

The class burst out laughing. The headmistress coughed and the silence was restored. She beckoned to the teacher to continue the conversation.

"Graceland? Where is Graceland?" continued Diane.

"Graceland is in a large forest. Marty knows all the corners of it.

My friends, the birds built me a large hut between four trees, a large nest where I eat fruit. I even made a barbecue." answered Annie.

In the room, the children put their hands on their mouths to prevent themselves from laughing. Only Gavin and Claire looked at her trustingly.

The headmistress went towards the teacher and stopped her with her hand.

"She needs a psychological evaluation. She is insane," whispered Mrs Crane to Diane who followed her in the corridor.

"No, Mrs Crane. Annie is very intelligent. And I think on the contrary that she must take the exams for the higher class. Her intelligence measure is very high, you saw yourself her results in mathematics. She must take the exams." objected Diane.

Mrs Crane added with anger without looking at Diane.

"In the mental institution. She will do the exams in the asylum."

The headmistress beckoned to the housekeeper to follow her and they disappeared in the corridor.

"Oh, no!" exclaimed Alan.

He howled in pain. A nurse entered the room and gave him an injection.

"Another injection! It is necessary that I flee from here," thought the Eagle.

Alan gave one blow of beak on the iron chain, a second, a third and he hurt himself. He got tired and laid down.

Alan wanted to close his eyes when he heard a noise on the window and he looked at the window.

"Marty! Hey Marty!" screamed Alan, happily.

The Jamaican Woodpecker was striking the wall with his beak.

After seeing that the wall was hard, he flew away higher and saw a window. Marty perched on the window and Alan saw him.

"Marty, hey Marty." called the Eagle.

Marty entered the room and moved towards the cage. The two birds greeted each other by intermingling their wings. Marty went to speak.

"Shush!" said Alan. He showed him the room. "The nurses are on this side. Speak quietly."

Marty jumped proudly on the cage and said aloud to him.

"The nurses are all gone and all is quiet."

"Calm! They are not gone. I just received an injection." murmured Alan.

"The last injection of the day. And you don't even know with what!" said Marty.

"I have been injected with a product which hurts a lot and makes me sleep." continued the Eagle. "Marty, I am pleased to see you. Now, tell me where are Annie's gold coins?"

"In a safe place!"

"A safe place? Which safe place?"

"Ardwick Green Park" said the Woodpecker with a serious voice.

Marty shook his head in front of the confused Eagle. He shook his wings to copy the movements of his head.

"Don't look at me like that. I made a small hole in a tree and I put the gold coins inside," continued the Jamaican Woodpecker.

"Oh, Marty! I gave you the order to return to Graceland and hide the bag there.

Not to put it in a place where the first person to come and put their hand in it will find the precious bag!"

"Nobody will know Marty's hiding-place. The detectors of the police won't even be able to find it. And then, it's not the most important thing at the Moment. We have to leave from here and find Princess Annie." Stated the Woodpecker

"You still did not listen to him!" said the disappointed Eagle.

He remained silent without a glance for Marty who started to worry.

"How did you know I was here?" asked Alan.

"Here comes Marty the great detective. You know, that is why Lucy likes me. I put my beak everywhere. I landed a few minutes after you and as I'm not so big, they didn't notice me. I saw you receiving the bullet in the shoulder and then watched you faint... "

Alan interrupted him.

"Marvel! And Marvel?"

"She wanted to take you while you were unconscious but the soldiers of the regiment, which is right beside the park intervened and brought you to the vet, to this house for animals. I simply followed you." continued the Woodpecker.

"And you didn't hide the bag?" Alan was irritated. "You told me that you had hidden it."

"I hid it after I knew where they took you. I followed you with the small bag in my beak."

"How long have I been locked up here? Marvel wants me dead at all costs." raged Alan.

"You have been here for more than three months. Marvel how do you know her?" asked the Woodpecker.

"Three months! It has been a long time," exclaimed the Eagle. "One day, I will tell you Marvel's history. I think that she knows I am here and has already found a means of assassinating me."

The birds looked around, they found objects broken close to the cage; they read the inscription on the bulbs.

"Morphine and Penicillin, Oh! The injections!" shouted Alan and Marty in unison as they opened their eyes widely.

"Marty, help me to remove the bandage. I just have to stretch out my wings and I will transform myself into a Parrot." said Alan.

The Eagle gave one, two, three, four blows of his beak on the knot of his bandage and he managed to undo the knot. Marty held the piece of the bandage firmly in his beak and started flying in the cage. He succeeded in unravelling the fabric which fell.

"Yippy, yippy." they shouted.

Alan went proudly to the middle of the cage and scoffed ironically at the Woodpecker, which looked at him, amused.

"Mister Marty the detective, I introduce Alan the magic Eagle to you." said the Eagle by bending the knee, happy.

Alan opened his wings and he transformed himself into a blue Parrot. He removed his leg in the chain and inspected his wing.

"I am cured. We can go now." shouted Alan proudly.

Alan and Marty left the cage, then the room they escaped through the window.

The birds were flying for hours without stopping. Marty went towards Alan.

"Alan, where are we going? If we only knew where Annie was?" asked the Woodpecker.

"An orphanage at Withington!" exclaimed the Parrot.

"Withington? But, we're going the wrong way. Withington is just before Disbury," the Woodpecker stated. "Just to ask me the way, don't forget that I am..."

"Marty the great detective! Yes, I know but I wanted simply avoid the crowds." replied the Parrot.

"There is no crowd to avoid. It is night already." continued the Woodpecker.

"The Eagle's shadow is shown like the day to the human."

"You are not an Eagle now but a Parrot. You can easily pass unnoticed."

"We are going to see the place now but tomorrow in the night, we are going back there to take Annie."

"Why not now?"

"She is not there!" exclaimed Alan.

"She is not there. And how is that? How do you know this?" began Marty again. "Don't forget that I am a..." said the Parrot as looked at the Woodpecker.

"A magic Parrot!" intervened Marty.

The birds pushed their beaks forwards and they emitted an acute noise of joy. They went to perch on the roof of a building.

"I am able to follow the movements of Annie and hear what she is saying by telepathy, I believe!" admitted the Parrot.

"Really!" exclaimed Marty.

"You can do the telepathy thing and tell me if Lucy and the children are well. If she misses me, if she is cheating on me."

Alan tended his beak and emitted a noise of joy. He turned around several times without a look at Marty.

"Mister the great detective does not know if his partner has cheated on him. You are pathetic." added Alan making fun of the Woodpecker.

"All jealous males are pathetic, the human ones too, aren't they Parrot!" screamed Marty.

"Who told you that I am human?" asked Alan, furious.

"I heard you speaking to Annie. I know your secret." admitted Marty.

Marty looked on his left and on the right then he saw the expression on the face of the Parrot. Alan had become red. The feathers, the wings, the beak and the legs had become red.

"Oooh, Alan! Look at yourself. You are red. Don't worry I can keep the secret. Stitched beak!" screamed Marty.

Alan opened his wings and saw himself red. He shook his body and he became blue again. He launched a cruel glance at Marty. He extended his wings and transformed himself into a Golden Eagle.

Alan threatened the Woodpecker with the beak. Marty moved away from him, fearing what could happen.

"Huh ! Don't eat me! Just because I know your secret doesn't mean I will shout it off the roof tops." said Marty, scared.

"Here is the shadow of the Eagle's claw," said Alan while looking at him.

By seeing the scared air of the Woodpecker, Alan started laughing. He rubbed his beak on the ground several time.

"I was joking."

It started to rain suddenly. Alan extended a wing and beckoned to Marty to shelter there.

"Manchester and the rain. What filthy weather!" said the birds simultaneously.

They pushed their beaks forwards and emitted a noise of joy. The rain was falling for nearly thirty minutes and Marty could not wait anymore, he asked Alan.

"What are we doing now?"

"We wait until the orphanage sleeps." answered the Eagle.

"Where is Annie?" asked Marty.

"In a Private clinic, a Psychiatric Department".

"What is she doing in the hospital for lunatics?"

"She is telling all the stories you told her in Graceland and her classmates, especially the staff at the orphanage believe she is insane."

"Poor little girl! Let's go and free her."

"No, we will do it tomorrow. There is a veranda on the roof of the orphanage, and we can ask Gavin to help... "

Marty did not give him the time to finish. He left the Eagle's wing and went into rain.

"Gavin! Who is this Gavin? Does Annie already have a boyfriend?" asked the astonished Woodpecker.

Marty could not believe his ears, he went back to hide under the Eagle's wing and screamed.

"Yippy."

"Marty, I won't allow my Grandaughter to have a boyfriend before her maturity." exclaimed Alan, serious.

"Oh, the jealous Grandfather!" said Marty, making fun of him.

Alan transformed himself into a Parrot. He remained pensive one moment without talking.

"We can go now. Everyone sleeps." said Alan.

"It still rains!" complained the Woodpecker.

"A bird does not always die because of the rain." continued the Parrot.

"But he becomes wet and gets cold." said Marty.

"Can he catch bronchitis also?" asked Alan, amused.

"This, you should ask to the vet." retorted the Woodpecker.

They flew a few miles then they perched on one of the orphanage windows. Alan and Marty looked through the window and saw children playing in a room. They were all boys. The Parrot recognised Gavin who was running after another boy. Alan touched the pane of the window with his wing and he knew that it was closed from inside. He jumped and went to land on another window beside it, but there was nothing he could do to open it.

A woman passed close to the room. The children heard the noise of her footsteps and they jumped on their beds pretending to sleep. The woman entered and saw the sleeping children. She switched off the light and left.

Alan recognised the housekeeper. Marty went round the building and found a window opened. He returned to the Parrot.

"This way!" said Marty.

Alan followed Marty and they entered the building by the window. They were in a corridor and Marty whispered to Alan ear.

"And now Mister Parrot. Do you know where we are and where we are going?"

The Parrot shook his beak and they continued wandering the corridor. They heard a noise coming from a room and stopped. A door opened and Joanne left. They were in the dormitory of the girls. Alan touched Marty on his wing.

"Annie's room is just there." said Alan.

"Where?" asked Marty.

"Where the little girl has just left," answered the Parrot while pointing his wing towards the door.

"Her name is Joanne. She spends her time bullying my Grandaughter. I want to taste her on my claws when I'm an Eagle." Joked Alan.

"Oh, Grandad!" exclaimed Marty.

"I was only joking!" laughed Alan. "But she has to stop bullying her classmates and I don't know why Annie didn't have the courage to tell the headmistress that she was bullied."

"You know that Annie has always been physically and mentally abused, maybe she thinks that the bullying is a normal thing," continued the Woodpecker.

"How do you know that Annie was physically and mentally abused?" asked Alan.

"Oh…I heard her saying something like that to her Mum Jane," lied Marty.

" And if you scratch Joanne, this will disrupt our plans!"

"There is always a plan B."

"Plan B? You have a plan B!" asked Marty, incredulous.

"I was joking." laughed Alan.

The little girl moved towards another corridor. They took another corridor in the opposite direction and they emerged in front of the boys' dormitory. Marty tried to open the door, which was closed. He started to strike the door with the beak. He put all his weight on the handle of the door and still did not manage to open it. Marty showed the door to the Parrot.

"This big door has almost broken my beak. It deserves a little magic potion," said the Woodpecker.

"Or the magic breath!" stated Alan.

He opened his beak and a blue smoke came out. The door opened suddenly and they entered inside the dormitory. Marty asked Alan.

"The woman, she switched off the light?"

"The children switched it on again. All the same! You know, they are all scared of the dark," answered the Parrot.

Alan went a direction and the Woodpecker followed him. Alan seemed to be looking for something. They stopped in front of a bed and Alan recognised Gavin. The Parrot reopened his beak blue smoke came out and went into the boy's nose. The boy stood up and went towards the door, which opened without a noise. The birds followed him. As soon as the Parrot saw that they were in a corridor, he beat his wings strongly and Gavin woke up. He wanted to scream after seeing the birds.

"Gavin, don't scream!" began Alan.

"Oh, you speak! You know my name!" exclaimed the amazed boy.

"All the Parrots I know speak," continued Alan.

Gavin stumbled and fell. He sat down and looked at the birds without understanding. The Parrot tried to reassure him.

"I know you're Gavin Knowles. My name is Alan and this is my friend Marty." introduced the Parrot.

"Marty! Alan!" cried out the boy who trembled all over his body. "Annie's friends! So she was telling the truth!"

"Yes. She was telling the truth." added Marty.

"He speaks too. The bird speaks too," wondered Gavin.

Marty beat his wings and landed on the knees of the boy. Marty was intrigued why Gavin was scared.

"Ah, you understand me. I am a Jamaican Woodpecker and I speak too..."

"It is not the time for long introductions. I want you to help us free my Grandaughter Annie." intervened Alan.

"Annie told us that her Grandfather was an Eagle," said Gavin.

"An Eagle-Parrot." admitted Marty.

"An Eagle-Parrot? That does not exist. I never saw one." continued Gavin.

"Alan, show him your gift," joked Marty.

The Parrot immobilised himself in the air; he opened his wings largely and transformed himself into a big Golden Eagle.

"Wow!" exclaimed Gavin, amazed.

"Now I want you to give me an answer. Will you help us bring Annie to the porch, tomorrow evening at the same hour?" asked the Eagle.

"How do you know about porch?" asked Gavin.

"Alan, didn't you give him a strong amount of the magic smoke? He asks too many questions." worried Marty.

"We need him." Said Alan.

"No, we don't." insisted the Woodpecker. "You could do the same thing to Annie tomorrow, to lure her towards the veranda with the magic smoke and we will take her with us. This boy has drunk Ginger wine. Look at him, he is drunk."

"Don't be too hard on him Marty," the Eagle defended the boy. "You were happy when you believed that Annie had a boyfriend."

"Oh, it's him! I've changed my mind he's crazy. He must be locked up in the asylum," joked the Woodpecker.

"Marty, the day my Grandaughter will marry this boy, I will transform myself into the ugliest bird in Graceland." said the Eagle.

"To whom do you refer to?" asked Marty.

"To Bill, of course." laughed Alan.

Gavin looked at them speaking without understanding. He fainted. Marty came close to him and touched him with his beak he turned the Eagle round.

"Do you have this effect on everyone? I don't know how Annie will ever get married in the future. You have just killed her latest date," said Marty.

Alan went close to the boy's head and he tried to tell if he was still breathing. "He's not dead he just fainted." admitted Alan.

"Fainted!" cried out Marty while falling.

He pretended to faint. The Eagle crossed the inert body of Gavin and poked Marty on the neck.

"It is time to go." growled the Eagle.

"What will happen to him?" asked Marty as he stood up.

The Eagle was about to answer, when a door opened abruptly, they met up face to face with a little girl who started to howl.

"An Eagle! An Eagle in the house!" shouted Joanne.

The birds scattered and fled. They dipped and ducked through the corridors, they did not recognise the way out so they found that they were lost.

They went round in circles in the orphanage. They heard people screaming in front and behind them. They rushed towards an open door and they flew into the room.

Alan recognised the headmistress office. He looked for the window and found it. He beckoned to Marty, showing him the way. They fled rashly. Alan did not have the time to see the electric wire which was in front of him. He bumped into the wire and he received an electric discharge. He fell like a stone.

Marty landed in haste. Alan fell close to the dustbins. Marty found Alan close to a dustbin, unconscious. He tried to shake the head of the Eagle but Alan did not open his eyes. Marty touched Alan's beak, neck and his wings, still nothing from the Eagle.

The Woodpecker cleared the rubbish on the Eagle's body and tried to lay his head gently on the ground. He walked around the Eagle and realised where they were.

"I shall rest first, I don't know how long it will take for Alan to wake up." said Marty to himself as he returned towards Alan.

The Jamaican Woodpecker flew into the dustbin to find something to eat. He found a potato and he emerged from the dustbin with the potato in his beak. He put it on the floor and he started to eat hungrily while making Alan as comfortable as possible.

Chapter 6 - The accident.

Claire Paxman found Annie alone lying in her bed in the girls' dormitory, she was unhappy. She went to sit close to her on the bed. She tried to comfort her.

"Annie my friend, you won't be unhappy all your life, will you? Don't worry if nobody believes you," said Claire. "I believe you, Gavin too. Isn't this the most important thing?"

Annie sat down on her bed while bending her legs, she looked at Claire who hugged her.

"I am sad because my Grandfather has gone. And I don't like this orphanage. I don't want to stay here anymore." cried Annie.

Claire tried to reassure her again and she said to her as she took Annie's hands between hers.

"Life is hard for everyone here in the orphanage but one day, you will find a family which will love you," she added while laughing as she pointed a finger at herself "Like me."

"Claire my friend, you are going? They found you a family?" asked Annie.

"Yes. I am going to Chester!" replied Claire. "Oh, don't be sad! We will see each other one day. You must promise me that, no matter what happens to you, you will fight don't let anyone walk all over you."

She looked at Annie's sad expression.

"My Grandmother Carla said a good little girl does not fight." bumbled Annie her head lowered.

"You must fight. You should not let Joanne hit you everyday and wait until your powerful Eagle comes to rescue you. You can even go and talk to the headmistress about the bullying." continued Claire.

"My Grandmother told me one day that violence leads to nothing." objected Annie.

"This is why you take all the punishment!" scolded Claire. She put her hands on Annie shoulders. "Come help me pack my bag. All the children at the orphanage are unhappy. Joanne's father never comes to see her and I think that he has abandoned her mother. She is right to feel anger."

"She at least had a dad," said Annie sadly. "I guess I have Marc, my Grandfather and Marty."

"There! You see, you are not alone in the world. Soon, you will also find a good family and you will move. Annie, I have a gift for you."

The little girl ran towards her bag and opened it. She gave Annie a little red haired rag doll. "Keep my doll safe," said Claire.

"Thank you very much Claire, it is the first time that someone offered me a beautiful doll. Can I also offer something to you?" asked Annie.

"Yes Annie, you can." answered Claire.

Annie went to open her suitcase; she took a pink dress out and gave it to Claire.

"This is the last dress my Grandmother gave me. Take it."

"Oh, it is beautiful!" Claire exclaimed as she took the dress.

"A dress with a lace hemline wow, I always dreamed of having a similar dress. You know what? I'm going to wear it now."

Someone knocked on the door and Annie went to open it. A woman entered and she looked at her intensely.

"Claire Paxman?" asked the woman.

Annie shook her head negatively and pointed at Claire who was dressing herself in the beautiful pink dress. Claire went close to the woman and bent her knee. The woman did nothing but looked at Annie intensely and touched her hand. She introduced herself to Annie.

"Paula Barlow. And you, what is your name?"

"Annie!" stammered the little girl.

"Mrs Barlow. My bag is ready." intervened Claire.

Mrs Barlow turned towards Claire, she threw a confused glance to her and she continued talking to Annie. She bent towards her.

"Annie, what have you done today?" asked the woman.

"Nothing interesting Mrs Barlow. I went to the school and we learnt about the populations of the world. Claire... "Called Annie. She laughed and took Claire's hand. "Claire gave me a rag doll."

They were interrupted by the voice of a man who entered the dormitory.

"Paula, is everything alright?" asked the man.

Paula went towards her husband and dragged him to the corridor. The two girls listened at the door. Claire grabbed Annie firmly.

"John, there is another girl in the room who I want. Can we change?" asked Paula.

"What are you talking about? Change! You know that adoption is very difficult in this country. We take the one we have chosen and we go." answered John.

The children heard them speaking and Claire started to cry. Annie left the room abruptly and went in front of the couple. John looked at her in surprise.

"Take Claire, she is a good girl. She is respectful and she does all her homework. Me, I'm stubborn, I'm good for nothing like Mrs Kirsty always said." began Annie, with her head lowered.

"Who is Mrs Kirsty?" asked Paula.

"She is... she is a bird which..., which lives in Graceland..." lied Annie.

"Where is Graceland?" Asked Paula while bending towards Annie.

"Paula, leave it!" suggested her husband after putting a hand on her shoulder.

"Is everything alright? Did Claire pack her bag already?" asked the headmistress who arrived behind them.

"Everything is alright. Claire is ready and we are leaving." answered John while going hastily towards the headmistress then he said to Claire "Love, where is your bag?"

The little girl remained paralysed. Annie ran into the dormitory and returned with Claire's bag and gave it to her.

"Claire, go! Your Dad and your Mum are waiting for you." cried Annie.

Claire took her bag and looked at Annie. The girls hugged and kissed each other on the cheek. John took Claire's bag in one hand and the other, he took her little hand.

"So Claire, you wanted to go away without saying goodbye?" asked Mrs Crane.

"Goodbye Mrs Crane!" replied Claire smiling at the woman.

The couple greeted the headmistress and they went away leaving Annie on the spot. Claire followed them. She turned towards Annie and waved her goodbye.

Alan felt like his head was leaving his shoulders. He stood up strongly and he shook his body.

"Oh, my head!" screamed Alan.

"I was wondering how long an Eagle would faint for." said a voice close to him.

Alan opened his eyes and saw Marty who was pecking at some seeds. He looked around him and they were close to several dustbins.

"An Eagle fainting, then a Parrot fainting?" continued the Woodpecker.

"Marty!" Alan exclaimed. "Since when have we been here?" asked Alan.

"I know only that it grew dark and now it's coming up to dawn."

"How did we arrive here?"

"You don't remember the accident. After the escape at the orphanage, you didn't see the electric wire, which was right in front of you, and you electrocuted yourself. I saw the flashes of lightening leave your body."

"Oh, Marty! I remember now. Is it too late to go to Annie?"

"It is nearly dawn and I don't know how we will do it. First, you must eat and change your appearance. Here are some fruits." said Marty.

Alan opened his wings widely and transformed himself into a Parrot. He started to rub his body with his beak. The Woodpecker was amused while looking at him.

"That's better!" confirmed Alan.

The Parrot shook his body and continued to stroke his feathers with his beak. "You look beautiful like that!" The Jamaican Woodpecker joked.

"Thank you." replied Alan.

"I want to go for a walk," continued Alan.

"No need to, I went and there are only vehicles circulating everywhere and not one park. We shall stay wedged behind these dustbins until the nightfall." explained Marty.

Alan jumped here and there without knowing what he was looking for. He flew and perched on a dustbin.

"Oh, my God! What is Annie doing now?" asked Alan, anxious.

"You're the expert, concentrate and you'll find her!" answered Marty.

The Parrot went down again to the level of the Woodpecker. He closed his eyes and concentrated he directed his energy and began to look for Annie. He did not receive anything. He tested without success. He opened his eyes.

"Marty, it's not working." said the Parrot.

"How is this? How is it not working!" exclaimed Marty.

"I tried, but I'm not able to connect to Annie. I didn't even have a vision. I don't see her anywhere." admitted Alan.

"No, you can't say that to me. Say some magic incantations." Ordered a confused Marty.

"I don't know any incantation. I do it all by concentration." explained the Parrot. "Then focus your energy towards Annie and you will find her. Try again!" continued an exasperated Marty.

Alan sat down on his legs and closed his eyes once more. He thought extremely hard about his Grandaughter.

"Annie, what are you doing now?" screamed Alan aloud.

A flash of lightening crossed his thoughts; Alan moved and opened his eyes. He closed them again suddenly and concentrated again. Marty shook him violently with his wings.

"Do you feel something?" asked the Woodpecker.

The Parrot didn't answer and remained perfectly still. Marty rotated around him looking at him with a curious glance.

"Annie! Make me know your thoughts." continued Alan loudly.

Suddenly, a flow of energy crossed him. He connected himself to the thoughts of his Grandaughter.

Annie, dressed in a pink dress, sat on the back seat of a car. At the front a man and woman. They were holding each other's hands. The woman turned towards the little girl.

"Don't worry Annie, we are your family now. We will never leave you. We're taking you to your new home, not far from here. In Chester, do you know Chester? It's a very beautiful place in the Northwest." explained the woman.

"No, I don't know Chester Mrs Barlow but I would like to live there with you. Are there any Parrots there? I would like to have one. I lost Mister my Parrot and I miss him." answered Annie.

"Darling, you will have any Parrot you like." continued the woman as she reassured the young girl.

"I want one with blue feathers and a yellow beak," added Annie then she addressed the Man at the wheel. "Dad, are we near Chester?"

"Don't worry, we're going to be there soon." answered the man.

Marty studied Alan without saying a word. He could not take it anymore seeing him without moving, he shook Alan. The Parrot opened his eyes in surprise. Alan got annoyed.

"Marty, you broke the transmission."

"What transmission?" asked Marty as he turned all around Alan.

"I was reading Annie's thoughts. She is on the road to Chester with a couple." howled the Parrot.

"Chester?" asked the Woodpecker. "What is she going to do there?"

"She is going to live there with this couple. She thinks that I am dead." said Alan sadly.

"Annie found an adoptive family!" exclaimed the Woodpecker, happily. "And afterwards?"

"Afterwards, nothing. You shook me." said the Parrot.

"No, no. You're going to concentrate again and have the image now. Find this car and we'll go there." ordered Marty.

"I am going to focus all my energy towards Annie but don't shake me!" said the Parrot.

Alan concentrated and he received only the thoughts of the little girl he found in the pink dress.

The journey to Chester. He opened his eyes and looked at Marty.

"Nothing!" growled Alan suddenly.

"What nothing?" Exclaimed the Woodpecker, "It is your fault.

We were about to take her yesterday at the orphanage but you insisted, you wanted to wait today. You will concentrate and find the vision even if I must peck you on the head a few times before you get something."

"I believe that it is the electric shock which turned everything upside down." recognised Alan.

"Then, you need another shock to put things right again." insisted Marty.

Without knowing what was occurring, Alan saw Marty flying away and landing at the edge of the dustbin. He looked into the dustbin and saw a small stick.

He entered the dustbin and re-emerged with the stick fixed in his claws.

Marty went to the level of the Parrot and dropped the stick. The stick landed on Alan's head.

"Ouch!" screamed Alan while rubbing the head.

"Now, see if you've found your visions. Find the vehicle on the road. Do you see Annie wearing a pink dress?" asked Marty now perched on the ground.

"You didn't have to drop the stick on my head. Ouch, it hurt a lot! But I will try again," stated Alan. He closed his eyes and began again aloud. "I must find the blue vehicle travelling towards Chester."

Alan directed his thoughts towards the blue car and a light spurted out of his head.

He was distinguishing clearly what was occurring in the car. The woman was howling, shouting to her husband to turn around and he refused. The little girl was sitting behind them. She was wearing a pink dress and a hat. A large bag was close to her she was hiding her face and Alan recognised only the pink dress.

"The pink dress that Carla had given to Annie." said Alan.

The man held the wheel firmly and looked hard at the woman who kept on howling.

"You don't need another child. We have already made our choice." said the man in anger.

The woman continued to howl, she tried to take the wheel. The man accelerated and hardly missed the other car, which came in front of them. Alan without knowing jumped. He flew away and Marty followed him,

"Alan, what happened? Where are you going?"

"Marty, Annie is in danger! The man at the wheel is driving without due care, he almost had an accident, let's go there! Let's follow them!" said Alan as he opened his eyes.

"Chester! I know the road, let us take this route," proposed Marty.

The birds flew higher in the sky. They flew a few miles when Alan stopped abruptly in the air.

"The Eagle goes quicker than a Parrot."

Alan extended his wings and became a Golden Eagle. He dashed as fast as he could in the sky.

"Wait for me!" screamed Marty.

Alan did not hear the Woodpecker shouting behind him, he was concentrating on what was occurring on the road.

The car was a small distance away now.

The woman was still howling and she slapped the man which caused him to lose control of the wheel and they collided with a truck which was coming behind them.

Alan had the time to see the woman and the little girl being thrown forwards by truck. They broke through the windscreen and their bodies fell down on the ground.

"Aaaargh!" howled Alan in full flight.

"Alan, what happened?" asked Marty.

The Eagle didn't answer, he disappeared in the sky and the Woodpecker lost sight of him. Alan landed in front of the broken vehicles. Without knowing, he transformed himself into an enormous Vulture, he became a dark black Vulture. The rage was burning in Alan's heart. The Vulture went towards the woman and chose not to attack her. He looked at the dead woman furiously, Alan started to scratch the ground instead, the black Vulture pierced the ground with all his strength and wounded his foot.

Marty landed and looked at the Vulture pricking the ground. He looked around him and saw the bodies. He recognised the pink dress.

"Annie!" screamed Marty "Alan, where are you? Annie had an accident. There is a black Vulture here."

"I am the black Vulture." said Alan as he walked close to him.

"Alan! What happened to you?" continued the worried Woodpecker, worried.

"Ask the woman! She killed my Grandaughter. She didn't stop badgering the man at the wheel," cried the Vulture while coming towards Marty.

"Marty, it's my fault. We arrived too late."

Alan flew away and went to throw himself against the truck. Marty followed him, he tried to reason him.

"Don't do it Alan!" begged the Woodpecker.

They heard the sirens of the police and the ambulances. Marty went to watch and he saw the vehicles coming towards the place of the accident at full speed.

"The police! Let's go." Screamed Marty.

"No, I want to see my Grandaughter for one last time." said the Vulture while returning towards the crippled body. "Oh, Annie! I didn't protect you. Oh, my God! What have I done? I killed Annie, I killed my Grandaughter."

Alan wanted to look at Annie when he heard gunshots. They were firing at him. The birds escaped from the police broken-hearted.

Alan was flying with rage in his heart. His rage slowed down he transformed into a Parrot, Eagle then into Vulture again. Marty followed him without intervening.

He saw that Alan was full of sorrow. He did not know where they were flying to.

The days and the nights followed one after the other without the two birds stopping. They were on and in the clouds. The Woodpecker looked around him and saw only white clouds. He wanted to see anything, but not another cloud. He plunged to the bottom, under the clouds and a violent wind shook him. He fought the wind and managed to balance himself.

Marty was continuing his race when he saw Alan taking to the skies swiftly. The Woodpecker went in the same direction as him. Alan had calmed down. Marty saw him transform himself into a Parrot. The wind dragged him viciously downwards. He drifted, letting the wind carry him.

The Woodpecker followed him at full speed. He stopped because he saw that Alan had regained the shape of an Eagle and rebalanced himself in the wind. Suddenly, Alan became a Vulture again and he continued his speed towards an unknown destination.

Marty decided not to leave him. They took again to the sky one after the other. Ahead of them, they saw a huge mass of immense rock.

Marty saw Alan moving towards the rock. When, he arrived above the rock, Alan let himself fall and the Woodpecker watched his body collapse on the large stone before entering water. Marty accelerated his speed and landed on the rock, he watched the Vulture disappearing into the water. Alan had fallen into the water.

Marty fought to pull him out of water.

Without success!

The Woodpecker succeeded in swimming and moving towards his right wing. He tried to pull him out and managed only to tear off a feather.

Alan transformed himself suddenly into a Parrot and Marty succeeded in taking him out of the lake.

Night began to fall. Marty stood by the edge of the crystal blue lake, close to the Parrot and he closed his eyes. He was tired and he fell asleep.

Marty the Jamaican Woodpecker woke up to find the Vulture still very still as if he was in a coma. He understood that Alan had changed his appearance. He went round him and touched him with his beak. Alan had his tongue out of his beak and his right wing completely broken. Marty looked around him and wanted to find a safe place. He flew without seeing a house. Tired, he returned towards Alan and found him in the same position that he had left him. Marty plunged his beak into the water and made the Vulture drink. Alan woke up and tried to stand up. Marty continued to make him drink water.

"The skin of a Vulture is hard you're lucky you didn't die. Don't move!" began the Woodpecker.

"Marty, what happened to me?" asked Alan.

"You have a broken wing," answered Marty, ignoring the question.

The Woodpecker went close to his head. "Change yourself into a Parrot."

"Why? Which form do I have now?" asked Alan.

"You looked like Bill." The Woodpecker joked.

"Bill! Now how is that?" asked the Vulture.

"You must stand up to see your new appearance and as your wing is broken, I suggest that you become a Parrot and cure yourself. First of all, try to open your wings largely." said Marty.

Alan tried to move and he was paralysed by a strong pain to his right wing. "Ouch, it hurts!" shouted the black Vulture.

Alan made a great physical effort and extended his wings. He bounced back on his legs into the shape of a Parrot and cured himself.

"Yippy, Yippy, Hurrah! Yippy, Yippy, Hurrah!" sang Marty with joy.

The Woodpecker started to dance all around Alan. The Parrot looked at him dancing without saying anything. Alan took his beak and started to stroke his feathers. Marty threw a glance to the Parrot and watched him clean himself up. Alan tried to concentrate and the Woodpecker stopped him.

"Alan, you promised to tell me the Marvel story." said the Woodpecker.

"Marvel! Marvel McCromarty?" asked the Parrot.

"What a funny name! Marvel, the greatest love of your life." continued the Woodpecker.

"In fact, she was the greatest love of my life. Marvel and me! We came from the same place and we studied in the same college. I fell in love with her immediately as she did with me. We promised to ourselves to stay together until the end of time." Began Alan.

"Oh, oh, oho!" laughed Marty.

"Everything spoiled itself when I introduced her to my mother who didn't like her at all. At the beginning, I didn't understand this hostility between them and then my mother explained to me that Marvel came from a family of witches. How they were witches from generation to generation! A history of transforming murderers." Alan told while advancing towards Marty.

"And how did your mother know it?" asked Marty.

"By her name. An ancestor of Marvel, Ian McCromarty, had married one of mine. That ended in the tragedy and a mysterious death.

My mother believed that I was going to finish in the same way and stopped me from seeing her again. As soon as Marvel knew, she threatened my mother and a few months afterwards, I learnt that my mother died the same way, her head cut off." continued the Parrot.

"Annie died the same way: a head cut off!" exclaimed Marty while jumping. Marty realised his mistake and wanted to correct it. "Annie did not die, Annie did not die."

"Annie is dead?" asked Alan suddenly. He started to beat his wings nervously and he asked again with rage. "Is Annie dead?"

Marty did not answer and Alan started to howl of pain. He changed himself into a black Vulture. As he was howling, he was increasing.

Alan became so big and dark that he obscured the landscape with his shadow. He closed his eyes and he found the vision, which showed him the accident again. Alan opened his eyes and they were red like small balls of blood.

"Marty, I could not save my Grandaughter." cried Alan calmly.

"You don't know if it was really Annie's body." said Marty to comfort him.

"I do not deserve to live. I do not deserve to live." continued the Vulture sadly. "Alan don't say that. Look find Annie with the visions! I believe that it is because of the electrocution at the orphanage. Too many events took place." objected the Woodpecker.

"I saw her in the car. I captured her thoughts. The pink dress! She was wearing the pink dress." retorted the Vulture.

"There are many pink dresses. Tell me a particular feature that you saw on the body of the little girl!" asked the Woodpecker.

"No, no..." howled the black Vulture.

"Annie had marks on her arms and I looked at the girl arms and she didn't have any of those marks." said Marty.

"I have lost the direction of my life. I will join her. I don't deserve to live, "
Cried the Vulture, broken-heartedly

Alan wanted to fly away and Marty barred the way. Alan gave him a peck on the beak, which sent the Woodpecker into the water pond.

Marty got out of the pond and went to perch on the back of the Vulture.

"Alan, do not despair! You can have your revenge on Marvel." said Marty without falling off his back.

"Why! Marvel has destroyed all the people I loved. Peter got married with her daughter. My little Annie is dead." cried Alan.

Large tears similar to large drops of rain ran out of his red eyes. Marty went down from Alan's back and tried to wipe the tears from Alan's eyes with his wing. Marty stared at Alan, but he could not hold his look because of the flames of anger in his eyes. The look of his eyes was similar to a volcano in eruption.

"Kirsty? Marvel's daughter! And why did you ask Marvel for help?" asked Marty to distract him.

"I didn't have anybody to turn to and I didn't think that she was going to ask me to belong her," explained Alan while staring at the Woodpecker. "Marty, go back. Go! Join Lucy and the children!"

"I am going nowhere without you!" screamed Marty.

"Go, Marty! Go away" continued Alan while attacking him. "I am bad. I will bring only evil to you. I couldn't defend my Grandaughter."

Marty wanted to speak and Alan jumped on him. The black Vulture positioned his large leg on the Woodpecker's neck and immobilised him. Marty didn't defend himself.

"I will kill you. Just like my dear sweet Annie. Go, Marty! Go away." cried Alan.

The birds did not see the shadow of another bird passing above them. The shade landed behind them and they heard.

"Nobody kills on my territory."

Alan and Marty turned towards the shade and they were face to face with a white Vulture, which was even bigger than Alan. They were looking at the King Vulture. The large bird had white feathers and legs, a red and yellow neck, at the bottom black feathers and a red beak. "The King Vulture!" screamed Marty while jumping behind Alan in fear.

The two Vultures gazed at each other lengthily and Alan saw the gleam in his eyes.

"Marvel!" said Alan.

Marty jumped around fearfully. The Vulture advanced majestically towards Alan. "Rory! My name is Rory." said the King Vulture introducing himself to his new found prey.

"Marvel's messenger! I see it in the gleam which shines in your eyes. Go ahead, what are you waiting for? Continue the work of the witch." howled Alan.

Without awaiting his answer, Alan jumped on the King Vulture and Rory did the same. They entered into a collision. Marty watched at them fighting for hours. Rory gained the upper hand quickly and Marty saw that Alan did not have the will to fight.

"Defend yourself. Alan, defend yourself!" shouted the Woodpecker.

Marty's cries made Rory furious. He succeeded in immobilising Alan on the rock and Alan could not fight anymore. The King Vulture took his powerful claws and firmly pressed them on Alan's neck.

Marty flew away and he went to land on the head of Rory. He scratched him with all his strength, he bit him violently.

Rory, with one of his wings, sent the Woodpecker flying. Before Marty reached the ground, Alan caught him with his wing. Alan had the time to catch Marty in full flight, but the Woodpecker fell on Alan.

The noise of Alan's body was heard on the rock. Marty freed himself from the black Vulture and wanted to speak to him. A blue smoke left Alan's beak and entered the beak of the Woodpecker. Without knowing what was occurring, Marty became a Parrot. He jumped several times on the spot. He looked at his feathers and they had become blue. He opened his wings for better look at his body, he transformed himself into a Jamaican Woodpecker. Rory flew towards them and gave Alan a final blow. Alan moaned, fell then fainted.

The King Vulture launched a cry of victory. He touched the body of Alan with his beak and his legs. After seeing that Alan was not moving anymore, he turned towards Marty and went towards him.

The Woodpecker moved back by jumping. He reached the pond of water and fell backwards. They heard an acute cry far off and Rory turned back. Marty saw him taking Alan by his claws and taking him away. Marty swam and left the pool of water. He shook his body and he removed the water. He flew towards them, he tried to follow Rory and Alan. He did not find any trace of them. They had disappeared. Marty turned back.

"Graceland," said the Woodpecker with sorrow. "I have to go back home. How will I give the news of Alan's death to the others? And with this appearance of a Parrot!"

The bird continued his flight with a heart inflated with rage.

Marty was flying for hours when he received an electric discharge in his head. He shook his head and continued his journey. Another flow of energy traversed his brain. It started suddenly to rain and the thunder muttered violently. Marty looked in the sky for a place where he could shelter. He went down under the clouds to discover a city a few miles away. The Parrot accelerated his descent.

"Where am I?" wondered the bird.

Marty landed and perched on a tree. He was flying between branches when he saw a light far off. He followed the light and he discovered that it had come from a house. The bird went to perch on the roof of the house. The rain was falling strongly and Marty was wet.

The Parrot found a dry place and went to sit on a window. Marty saw a sign and did not believe his eyes. He landed on the sign.

"In the United States. I am in the United States!" screamed the Parrot.

The thunder muttered again and the flashes split the sky. Marty received another electric discharge. He fled, he took refuge on another window, which he found open and he entered. He went to land on a bedside table. Marty shook his body to remove the water and he closed his eyes.

The flash passed into his head and Marty believed to see Annie playing in a school playground. She was running behind a boy and Marty recognised Gavin; he opened his eyes and shook his body.

"Annie is alive!" screamed Marty.

Marty did not believe his vision. He strongly shook his head and focused all his energy towards Annie. The little girl was running behind Gavin and was trying to catch him. She wanted to take something from him. She twisted Gavin's hand and opened it. She took an object and Marty saw a ball.

The school bell rang and all the children placed themselves in row in front of the headmistress who was holding a handkerchief in her hands. She cleared her voice and addressed herself to the children.

"I have a bad news to announce to you.

Claire Paxman your classmate who was adopted by the Barlows' died tragically in a car accident, two weeks ago. I have just had the news,"
There were cries amongst the children. Mrs Crane clapped her hands and she calmed the children.
"The couple also died and there was a Vulture near the place of the accident. We don't know if they wanted to avoid the Vulture on the road. We will all gather in the vault and we will request a prayer for their souls."
She wiped her eyes with the white handkerchief.
The children entered the classroom in silence. Marty saw Annie wiping a tear off the back of her hand, she was crying. He felt a tear running out his eyes. He could now understand the pain of Alan until now. Annie stepped aside from the rows and took another direction. Gavin followed her and took her in his arms. He comforted her by tapping her shoulder gently.
"Don't cry Annie, everything will be alright like before."
"Nothing will be like before. I lost my friend. My Grandfather died, my Mum too. All that I love dies. I hate myself. I hate you too." shouting the little girl while pushing him.
Annie ran away. Marty was filled with sorrow and anger. He saw Annie squatting by herself in a corner of the playground she crying endlessly.
"Annie, my little princess, I am coming. Your Grandfather is coming." cried Marty with a sharp voice.

The Parrot left the room at great speed and flew away.

Marty felt that he was not flying quickly. He suspended himself in the air, he extended his wings and became a Golden Eagle. He took his journey at the speed of the wind. He made some aerobatics in full flight.

"This is better!" screamed the Golden Eagle.

Marty flew straight as an arrow in the sky and flew through the clouds. The wind made him lose his balance; he extended his wings to rebalance himself.

He disappeared in the sky like a spectre in the night.

Chapter 7 - Marty the great.

Annie sat in front of her plate of food in the refectory. She was not eating. Joanne was not far from her and she was looking at Annie with her eyes mixed with envy and hatred. Annie put her head between her hands on the table and watched the floor. She was thinking about her Grandfather. She heard Joanne saying.

"Little whiner! You're always crying your defender is dead eaten by a Vulture." Laughed the little girl.

"Don't you dare speak about my friend." shouted Annie as she rose.

Joanne left her seat and went in front of Annie. She pointed a threatening finger at Annie; it brushed harshly against her face.

"What are you going to do?" asked Joanne.

Annie sat down without answering her question; she lowered her head and looked at her plate.

"I'm the only one in charge now. Nobody eats without my permission," continued Joanne. She took Annie's plate. "Miss bird lover, ask me for permission to eat."

The children started to shout.

"Joanne rules! Annie sucks! Joanne rules! Annie sucks!"

Annie raised her head; she stood up and confronted her as she starred intensely at her. Annie's cheeks ballooned with anger.

She looked at Joanne more seriously but sat down once again.

"And why would I ask your permission?" enquired Annie.

"Oh, oh, oh, someone is growing up!" Joanne said mockingly.

The group of children that had surrounded them laughed at Annie. The children continued shouting.

"Joanne rules! Annie sucks! Joanne rules! Annie sucks!"

Annie pointed a challenging finger at Joanne who moved back a few steps, not believing the bravery of the little girl.

"Put my plate back where it was, on this table." said Annie to Joanne who finally started laughing.

Joanne looked at the other children who continued to make fun of Annie.

"Make me put your plate on the table." shouted Joanne while watching Annie rise once more.

Annie sat down again and she positioned her hands on the table. Joanne laughed even more, she took the food, which was in the plate and poured it on Annie's head. Annie rose and punched her in the face.

"Fight, fight. Fight, fight," shouted the children. "Fight, fight. Fight, fight."

The little girls clutched one another and fought doggedly. Annie gained the upper hand quickly and pinned the head of Joanne on the table.

She started to scream and everyone could hear her in the corridors.

"Mum, Mum." cried Joanne.

One girl clutched Annie by the hand and another intervened. Suddenly, everyone was fighting.

Katie Pickles and the headmistress entered the refectory in a hurry. They found the girls fighting and Mrs Crane took a whistle from her pocket and blew on it. The children stopped fighting immediately.

"What is going on here? Everyone is in detention. Go to your rooms now!" screamed Mrs Crane.

The children fled and they scattered into the corridors leading to their rooms.

Gavin was on the balcony of the refectory, he saw Annie fighting and he was proud of her for standing up for herself. He ran into the corridor, he waited until she passed near him and called her. The children went back into the refectory. They found it empty. Gavin took Annie under a table and they sat down. The boy gave her a friendly pat on the shoulder.

"If Claire was here she'd be proud of you, I'm sure she saw it all wherever she is. Today, you stood up to your fear, Annie."

Annie put her head on the shoulder of Gavin who hugged her strongly.

"You really believe Claire is proud of me at this moment?" asked the little girl while Gavin nodded in agreement.

"I also want my Grandfather to be proud of me. I lost him too. Do you believe that they would agree that I join them?"

"Why do you want to join them, Annie? Your Magic Parrot is not dead. I saw him," said the boy. "Marty too."

Annie opened her eyes widely. Gavin laughed at her eyes all rounded with surprise. She wanted to shout with joy. Gavin lent towards her to close her mouth with his hand as he did so he knocked his head against the table and Annie laughed at him. He sat close to her once again.

"Tell me, where did you see them?" asked Annie.

"They came here looking for you, Marty and him, a few weeks ago. I was sleeping in my room when I found myself suddenly in the corridor, when I opened my eyes. A Parrot asked me to take you to the veranda where we were the other day with Claire. I was amazed."

Annie put her hands on her mouth to prevent herself from screaming. Gavin smiled as he saw Annie putting her two hands over her mouth.

"Marty spoke to me too. They knew my name. After, I fainted and awoke in the orphanage infirmary. I thought about it and I know that it was not a dream. I told Claire before she left and she believed me." added Gavin.

"Oh, Gavin! Thank you so much for telling me that, I am happy for my Grandfather. He's not dead. I will pray that I will see him one day."

"Fate will answer all your wishes. My father always said that..." Gavin stated with a smiling.

"Gavin, you've got a dad?" asked Annie, curious.

"Had a dad! But my father was a bad man and he did odd things to me. After my mother left him for another man, he started drinking and hitting me. He blamed me for his sorrow; he told me that it was my fault my mother left with another man. That their lives were good before my birth! And he began really hurting me. He locked me up in a room and gave me neither drink nor food during my days," Gavin told his story with tears in his eyes. "One day, I finally escaped. I wandered for days and days. I learnt how to steal from the pockets of people in the streets."

"No, Gavin!" said Annie. "My Grandmother Carla always taught me that stealing from people is wrong. Stealing and swearing are not good for a child."

"I didn't have the choice. My father had too much money but his son had to steal from the pockets of the poor so that I could survive." explained Gavin.

"Swear that you will never steal again." said Annie.

"Swear for what?" asked the boy.

"For stealing..." answered Annie.

She took his hands in hers. She saw his answer on his face and Gavin started laughing.

"I don't steal anymore. Here at the orphanage, it's not perfect but I'm happy. I was forced to grow up quickly I haven't really had a childhood." stammered the boy.

"You're only ten years old." continued Annie.

"Almost eleven and older than your Grandfather," playfully mocked Gavin. Both children started laughing loudly.

They heard a noise suddenly coming from the door of the refectory and they calmed down. They went under the tables looking for an exit. They emerged in the kitchen and they heard the noise for the second time. The noise was coming from the ceiling. They looked up and saw a bird flying.

Marty the Parrot was looking for the girl's dormitory. He could not remember the way because all the corridors looked the same.

"Oh, my Princess. My little Annie, where are you?

He stopped one moment and grabbed the curtains of the window with his claws. Marty closed his eyes firmly and concentrated. His vision showed him the room in which she was. The bird left the curtains and whirled to the kitchen of the refectory. Marty looked at the bottom and saw the children.

"Annie! Annie!" screamed the blue Parrot.

Marty went down and landed on a table close to her. Annie wanted to scream, Gavin put his hand on her mouth and whispered to her.

"Don't scream Annie, it's your Parrot."

Gavin showed his arm and Marty came to land on it. The boy led Annie and the Parrot into the corridors silently. They reached the large veranda.

After seeing that they were out of sight, Gavin leaned his arm towards Annie and gave her the bird.

"Princess Annie, here is your Parrot." said Gavin. Annie picked up the bird in her hands and gave him a cuddle. She kissed him wildly under the amused eye of Gavin. He was happy for Annie.

"Oh, Grandfather! Where have you been?" asked the little girl.

Marty stuck his beak close to Annie's mouth, He returned her kisses as he made soft sounds in the air.

"I flew here and there, looking for you," said the Parrot.

"Oh, Mister Grandfather!" Annie was annoyed. "It's not worth thinking of my beautiful Parrot."

Marty left her arms and went to sit on the edge of the veranda. He walked proudly under the amused eye of the boy who approached him.

"I wanted to tease you. I see that you are fine. Now, let's go!" said Marty.

He opened his wings and he became an enormous Golden Eagle. He landed on the floor and said to Annie.

"Jump on my back, we're leaving."

"Where are we going Alan? To Graceland?" asked Annie. Marty did not answer and she said to the boy. "Gavin, come with me."

Annie jumped on the back of the Eagle. She drew the boy by the hand and he went up behind her. Marty flew towards Ardwick Green Park and landed in a rushed manner.

"We cannot go to Graceland with this child." began Marty as he directed a glance at Gavin.

"Gavin is my friend and he doesn't have any family like me." said Annie lowering her head. "He's got a father, but he fled his house because his dad was hurting him."

"Oh, Annie! I take responsibility for you alone," thundered Marty. He looked at the children. "We will find Gavin's father."

"No! I don't want to go back home. I don't want to see him. I'd prefer to return to the orphanage." shouted Gavin.

"Shush! We cannot return to the orphanage now. It is dark and we must find somewhere to sleep. But first, wait for me." added Marty not wanting to discuss this with the children.

He transformed himself into a Parrot and flew around the park. He went to perch on a branch. As soon as he saw that the children were not looking at him, Marty changed into a Jamaican Woodpecker and put his head in a hole. He pulled out the bag of gold coins. He changed himself into a Parrot once more; he went in front of Annie and Gavin. Marty gave the bag to the little girl.

"My gold coins!" exclaimed Annie.

"What would you say about a good meal?" asked the Parrot.

"Great!" replied the children.

"Then jump on my back." said the Parrot.

Marty turned and showed them his back with his beak.

He transformed himself into a Golden Eagle again and the children jumped on his back. Marty flew away quickly.

The Eagle flew over the city in search of a shop. All were closed. He was about to turn back when he saw a shop open. Marty landed in the corner of the street.

"Now, who is courageous enough to go shopping? Somebody has to speak to the shopkeeper and buy food. We have a long road in front of us." said the bird.

"To buy something in the shop, we need money, don't we?" began Gavin while gesturing at the Eagle.

"Good point!" said Marty. He turned towards Annie. "Give me two gold coins."

She took the coins from the bag and gave them to Marty. He blew on the coins and changed them into banknotes.

"Forty pounds!" screamed Annie.

"Give the banknotes to Gavin and he will buy food." said Marty.

The boy took the money and went towards the shop. He opened the door and entered. The man behind the counter looked at the little boy going round the shop with suspicion. Gavin had a basket in one hand and took bread, cheese and a litre of milk. Gavin saw sweets and he took a pack. He began to walk back to the shop counter, but he knocked himself against the shopkeeper.

"What are you doing outside at this hour of the night? Where are your parents?" asked the shopkeeper.

Gavin looked at him in confusion. He wanted to pass, but the man barred the way.

"Kid, do you have money to pay for all that or are you a little robber?" said the shopkeeper.

Gavin gave him a banknote for twenty pound. The shopkeeper snatched the banknote out of the hand of the boy. He went behind the shop counter and opened his till. The man looked at the boy even more suspiciously.

"What are you doing alone outside at this hour?" asked the shopkeeper again.

"I am not alone, I am with my Grandfather and my sister. They are outside." Gavin answered with his eyes lowered.

"Outside! Why didn't your Grandfather come to buy food himself? He preferred to send you." continued the shopkeeper.

The boy defended himself.

"My Grandfather sent me because my sister was not feeling well."

The man closed his till carefully and gave the change to the boy who put it in the pocket of his trousers. Gavin left and the shopkeeper followed him. Marty was following the scene carefully.

"Annie, hide behind this large dustbin. Come out only if I call you." said Marty to the little girl.

Annie went behind the dustbin. Marty looked around him and saw that Annie was not looking at him.

He opened his wings and transformed himself into an old woman. She went towards Gavin who was coming towards her.

"Well done my darling, you were fast." exclaimed Marty.

Gavin was surprised meeting the old woman and looked at her curiously. She was walking with difficulty.

The shopkeeper was looking at her behind the boy.

"Madam, are you with this child?" asked the shopkeeper, anxiously.

"Yes, I know him. He's my grandchild," answered Marty.

"I saw him alone and I was scared of someone attacking him at this late hour of night. That is why I followed him to see whether there was somebody with him." added the shopkeeper.

The man turned back as he saw someone entering his shop. He gave a small slap to Gavin on the shoulder.

"I am going back to my shop. Do you need anything else?" asked the shopkeeper.

"Don't worry! Everything is alright." replied the old woman.

The shopkeeper went to enter his shop, however he hesitated and went back towards them.

"You told me that you were with your Grandfather and your sister?" asked the shopkeeper to Gavin.

"I wanted to say my Grandmother and my sister, but I was scared." stammered the boy.

The man looked at them then entered his shop. Marty took Gavin's hand.

As soon as they reached the dustbin, Marty called to Annie who did not answer. They went behind and found her asleep on the ground. Marty lifted the little girl and carried her on her shoulders. She asked Gavin to follow her. They went along the street and stopped in front of a motel.

Marty went to the reception to book a room.

"I want a room with a double bed for me and my Grandchildren. They are hungry and tired," said Marty pointing at Annie with her finger. "They deserve a good night of sleep."

"Thirty five pounds for the room!" said the receptionist.

Marty turned towards Gavin and asked him for money which he took from his pocket. Gavin gave the receptionist some money and picked up the room key.

"Second floor, second door on your right." added the woman.

Marty and Gavin went up in the room gently while carrying Annie. They put the little girl on the bed and covered her with a blanket.

The old woman opened the bag of provisions and took bread and milk. She gave them to Gavin.

"Eat now, the road will be long tomorrow." she said to him, calmly.

Gavin sat down on the bed and started to eat as he looked at the old woman who moved towards the window. She remained there staring out of the window for a long time.

When she turned towards Gavin, he was already sleeping on the bed. She came towards him and pulled up the duvet cover over his chest. She sat down on a chair close to the door and fell asleep too.

"Aaargh! Aaargh!"

The Vultures were shouting while turning all around Marvel's house. The sinister birds emitted acute whaling cries. They were hungry and they were everywhere, on the trees, the windows and in the house. Marvel's hair swirled in the wind, she moved towards a large caldron that was on a fire and she plunged two big human body parts into the caldron. She went towards a table where Alan was lying. She went in front of him.

"Here comes the moment that I have been waiting for," said the witch as she starred at the black Vulture. She shouted for joy.

"Your mother is not here anymore to split us up. You will belong to me forever."

Marvel touched Alan's body with her long nails. She wanted to be sure that he did not move.

"Ah, aha, aha! Here you are, finally! Beautiful man of my dreams.

For generations, I have tracked you. Aha aha, aha!" laughed the witch while walking around him.

Marvel shook his head and his wings. She opened her wings largely, then her face and body changed appearance. She became older, thinner.

She appeared to have more than a thousand years upon her. Someone knocked on the door abruptly.

"Who is it?" asked the witch.

"Prior!" answered an Eagle.

"Come in!" Continued the old woman.

Marvel opened the door with the power of her mind. A Bald Eagle entered the house and bent his knee in front of the witch.

"I am waiting for your orders!" he said.

"Go to Graceland. I have left you as King and do not let the prisoners' flee." ordered the old woman while approaching him.

"And Marty?" asked the Bald Eagle.

"Kill her!" answered the witch without hesitating. Prior bent his knee and left the house. Marvel turned towards Alan and licked his face. She went all over his body with her tongue. As she advanced towards his legs, her head changed. She became a very long, large snake, a python. She opened her mouth largely and started to swallow Alan starting with his head.

Marvel had almost swallowed half of Alan's body when the door opened abruptly. The King Vulture entered and went close to Marvel. The witch withdrew from Alan's body with one stroke and put her head upright. The snake filled the room with her body. It advanced towards Rory who was not scared at all, the snake pushed out her long tongue. Rory recognised it was Marvel; he distinguished her two pointed teeth which were shining.

"What do you want?" Asked the big snake

"The smoke. He does not have it anymore." answered Rory as he pointed at Alan with his wing.

"What!" screamed Marvel.

"He had the time to give it to his wife, Marty." added the King Vulture while trembling.

Marvel transformed herself immediately into an old woman and opened the beak of Alan. She whiffed the air and nothing left.

"Without this magic, we cannot be united for eternity!" howled Marvel in rage. "How did you take him here without the breath? Blasted fool! You never obey the orders. I must always do everything by myself."

"Majesty, he still had the breath in him when I broke his neck." said the King Vulture.

Marvel furiously, moved in the room. She jumped on the neck of Rory and began to twist it then increased her pressure.

"Oh, yes! And how doesn't he have it anymore? Without the breath, I cannot continue my ritual. I want this smoke! Aaaaargh!"

Marvel howled in pain and twisted her body nervously.

"Majesty..." Rory wanted to say something.

Suddenly Marvel changed herself into a Turkey Vulture. Marvel bounced on Rory and sent him flying against the wall with her wing. The turkey Vulture savagely bit Rory, which helped him escape. The King Vulture managed to open the door and fled.

The Turkey Vulture transformed herself into an old woman and did not pursue Rory. She emitted an acute scream and all the Vultures, which were in the neighbourhood came towards the house. They perched everywhere in and outside the house. They all bent their knees towards Marvel.

"Prepare yourself for war!" ordained Marvel.

Rory made course to regain the power of three. He flew for hours in search of Marty. He slowed down because of his wound on his wing. He saw a tree, he sat on a branch and he started to search his feathers of his body with his beak. He thought that he had to find Marty at all costs. He sat down on his legs, closed his eyes and concentrated.

"Marty, let me see you." said the Vulture.

Rory received a flow of energy suddenly into his head and he followed the vision. A blue light led him through the cities until reaching a point. He saw Annie and Gavin who were holding each other by the hand and were walking between the arrays. They were in an outdoor market near a park of attractions. It was a sunny day and the place was lively. Rory did not see Marty. He shook the branch on which he was sitting and concentrated.

Gavin took a silver coin from his pocket and bought a doll. He gave it to Annie.

"I don't want to see my father." began Gavin.

"I don't think that you're going back to live there. I want only to see your castle. I've never seen a castle before." begged Annie.

"I was there a long time ago. I don't know the way anymore." said the boy.

Annie threatened him with a finger.

"Ooooh, Gavin! Tell the truth!"

"I don't want anybody to recognise me." admitted the boy while lowering his glance.

"Nobody will recognise you, we will go unnoticed." continued the little girl with a soft voice.

"We'll go unnoticed with your Eagle!" shouted Gavin without smiling.

"We can ask my Grandfather to drop us close to the castle. We will go there alone. Look, no one will recognise us there." said Annie.

Gavin went for a walk close to a tree. He sat down and called Annie with his hand.

"If my father sees me, he would beat me."

"Don't worry about that. My Grandfather will jump on him and your father will run scared." She replied while laughing.

Annie started wincing, wincing like someone in pain. Gavin also started laughing.

"We must first ask my Grandfather's permission." mumbled Annie.

"We cannot make him come down from the tree now. Everyone will see a blue Parrot," said Gavin.

The children raised their eyes to the tree where Marty had sat. They looked at the Parrot, which greeted them with a wing.

"I hear you," said Marty on the tree. "From Sheffield to Narborough, it is far. We will travel at nightfall."

"Alan, you are the best!" screamed the children with joy.

Gavin stood up and drew Annie by the hand, they moved away from the tree leaving Marty to his thoughts.

"Let us ride the wooden horses at the amusement park." suggested Gavin.

The children ran towards the park. Gavin took two coins and gave them to a park staff, they opened the small door. Gavin picked up Annie to put her on a wooden horse and he took the other next to her. The Carousel started revolving.

Rory opened his eyes widely and flew away. He slowed down and concentrated in full flight. He followed his vision and let himself be guided by it.

The Carousel was revolving and Annie's hair was blowing in the wind, she was laughing. Marty looked at her sadly.

"Oh, lord! In all my life I have never seen her so happy. That is why I should not tell her about her Grandfather's death. Alan, what have you done? I could not tell you that I was Carla, your wife." said Marty as she closed her eyes. "No…no, I am Marty, the Jamaican Woodpecker and I will remain this way until my last days. How could I return in this world where everyone knows that I am dead and buried?"

Marty jumped from branch to branch and continued his meditating; he had a really bad headache and touched his head with one wing.

"Alan my love, you didn't die in vain. You gave me this power which will enable me to free all the slave birds of Graceland," continued Marty raising a leg and scratching his head.

"Poor Lucy, I was her best friend since Marvel locked us up in the high prison in her castle and we adopted our three little orphans. I carried out my own survey, we inhabitants of Graceland are all human, we are all men, women and children transformed into birds and all slaves of Marvel."

Marty remembered Alan calling him Marty the detective. Marty emitted an acute cry of sadness.

"Poor Alan! I saw him jumping on Mortal and beating him. He saved my life. What a miracle! Oh! I lost him again. Now, there is Annie and I have to take care of her." continued Marty.

The Parrot looked at the sun which was setting and thought about the children. They had to leave. He looked at Gavin, Marty had appreciated his courage and bravery in the shop. He continued in his thoughts.

Gavin kept the secret. The boy did not tell Annie that he transformed himself into an old woman. Marty flew away and went to sit on the shoulder of Gavin. He asked them.

"How was your day, children?"

"Good! The day was good." answered the children.

They went in silence. Marty left the shoulder of Gavin to land on the ground. He transformed himself into a Golden Eagle.

"Jump on! We are not going to Narborough on foot." joked Marty showing his back with the beak.

Rory opened his sinister eyes and flew away, he accelerated his pursuit, he was not far from his enemies now he thought. He went up in the sky and hid near a cloud, he saw Marty flying. Rory went on the cloud and raised his leg. He brought his claws to his beak and sharpened them. He did the same with his left leg. He was ready to fight.

The King Vulture sprung out of the cloud and took again to the sky on his vengeful pursuit. He looked Marty, but he could not see him anymore. The Vulture closed his eyes for a moment and saw Marty going down to a castle. They arrived at Narborough. Rory watched from a branch close by and sharpened his claws again. He closed his eyes and focused all his energy towards Marty. He followed the vision.

Marty dropped Gavin and Annie off in a large garden and went to perch on a fence. The castle of the Duke of Narborough extended majestically and large lanterns were lighting the surrounding area. Marty beckoned to Gavin and Annie showing them that the way was free. The children passed through the big garden. They found a door opened and entered the big castle. They emerged towards an alley.

Gavin held the hand of Annie firmly and directed her towards a door, which he opened. The library was roomy and was lit by a chimney fire. He advanced towards a portrait fixed on the wall.

"Here is my mother. The woman who abandoned me." introduced the boy sadly.

The little girl distinguished the features from the woman of the portrait and looked at Gavin.

"You look like her..." said Annie as she reflected on the image of the painting. Gavin did not listen to her speak, he searched the room and went towards a wall where he pressed a stone in the wall. Another door opened and he went inside the room. He took a book and went out quickly.

"Annie, let's go!" shouted Gavin.

The little girl stood still in front of the portrait. She did not hear Gavin speaking to her. He came and took her hand. He dragged her out of the library by force. The children reached the stairs and Annie knocked her foot against the step. They heard a male voice coming from a room at the top of the stair.

"Gavin, is that you Gavin!" asked the man.

"Mr Knowles, Gavin will never return. You know that well. It is the cat. Try to take your medicine." said a woman.

The children continued on their way while investigating. When they got outside of the castle. They started to run in the garden.

"Can we stop now." begged Annie who was exhausted from running.

"Let's go, Annie." ordered Gavin.

Annie stood up, she raised her eyes and looked for the Parrot. They heard a noise of beating wings behind them.

"Are you looking for me?" asked a voice.

Gavin went in front of Annie. They saw the King Vulture and they were petrified. "Who are you?" asked Gavin.

"Mister Grandfather!" answered Rory mockingly.

Marty was scratching his legs with his beak when he had a vision of the danger. He raised his eyes and saw Gavin fighting against a Vulture while Annie hid behind him.

"A Vulture! It is impossible!" screamed Marty.

He flew towards them. Marty landed and transformed into an Eagle in front of the Vulture. He stared at the bird and saw a gleam in his eyes. The birds measured themselves against each other.

"I came back to kill you, Marty." said the King Vulture.

The large Vulture danced on his legs and showed him the claws. Marty read his thought and recognised him.

"Rory, the messenger of Marvel!" continued Marty without fear. He turned towards Gavin. "Take Annie away from here. I will handle the situation."

"You will handle the situation! You will handle the situation." howled the King Vulture

Rory got angry and he stared at Marty.

Gavin saw Marty extending his wings majestically and become a Parrot. The boy covered the face of Annie with his hands. Rory went towards Marty.

"Like that, you don't have control of your power. I came to take the breath that Alan gave to you. Give it back to me or I will take it by force." threatened Rory.

"Come take it!" said Marty after placing a leg ahead ready to fight.

Rory opened his wings and sprang towards the Parrot. Marty jumped and landed far from Rory. The King Vulture started again and Marty flew. He went and landed on Rory's back.

"Roxanne, transform! You're not a Vulture but a little girl." begged Marty.

The Vulture turned over savagely. He shook his body and Marty fell abruptly. Rory gave him a wild blow with his beak, but the Parrot dodged it. Marty jumped in the air, he opened his wings and transformed himself into an enormous Californian Condor.

"Oh, you do know how to use your powers! You've learnt how to use the breath. You will also learn how to give it to me." growled Rory.

The birds extended their wings and entered a collision. They fought wildly. They changed themselves into blacks Vultures. Annie freed herself from Gavin and fled. The boy followed her and caught her.

"I must help my Grandfather." screamed Annie.

The boy held her firmly. Annie bit his hand and Gavin howled with pain. She took advantage of the situation and ran towards the birds.

"No, Annie stay with me." shouted Gavin as he shook his hand.

The little girl ran and Gavin followed her. She looked for a stick; Annie did not find a stick and wanted to throw herself on the Vultures. She looked at both of them and saw that they were Black Vultures. She looked, but could not tell them a part. Gavin reached for her and held her against him so that she could not intervene with the fight.

Rory and Marty were still fighting when Annie started to shout impatiently.

"Go ahead Alan. Beat him, you can do it! Beat him."

Marty dodged a violent blow from Rory's beak. He took his neck, rolled it and managed to pin Rory to the floor. Annie continued to shout.

"Alan, you can beat him!"

The birds struck each other's wings. Rory managed to free himself from Marty's' hold. They gave each other violent blows with their beaks. Rory jumped behind and lost his balance. He transformed himself into a King Vulture once more. Marty did not leave him time to stand and jumped on his head. He put his legs on his head and pinned Rory to the ground again. Annie bent herself towards the battle; she bit Gavin on the hand again and sprang towards the Vultures.

She threw herself on the King Vulture; she held his legs and his wings firmly with her entire body. He stopped moving.

Marty immobilised the head of the King Vulture and opened his beak with his claws. Marty let escape a violet smoke from his beak, which entered Rory. The King Vulture transformed into beautiful Caribbean girl. Around ten years old, Annie fell behind Marty, petrified. Gavin joined her.

"It's finished now! I overcame Rory," said Marty to the children. "Now, we have to cure Roxanne to prevent her from following Marvel's call."

"Marvel! Do you believe that it's Marvel who sent her?" asked Annie.

"Marvel! Who is Marvel?" asked Gavin.

"It's too long a story for now. Hold her firmly. I must give her the three breaths so that she can be cured completely." replied Marty.

Gavin laid Roxanne down on her back; Annie helped by holding her arms. Annie opened Roxanne's mouth with her hands allowing Marty to blow inside the little girl's mouth.

"The breath of the Vulture... The breath of the Eagle... The breath of the Parrot..." said Marty while changing simultaneously into an Eagle then into a Parrot.

Roxanne coughed and awoke. She sat up, she looked at the Parrot and the children.

"Where am I? My mother, my father..." said Roxanne.

"All is right!" said Gavin as he took a close look at her.

"We must find a place to sleep. Tomorrow, we are going back to Graceland. I have a job to do there." suggested Marty.

Already, he moved towards the castle. The three children followed him. Gavin went in front to direct them into the castle. Gavin led them to a room and he closed the door behind the Parrot.

"I believe that it's better to spend the night here." said Gavin.

"Who does this room belong?" asked Annie.

"It's mine! Oh, I forgot my book. The gold coins..." replied the boy. He searched his body and he felt a bump in his pocket. "The coins are in my pocket but I lost the book."

Marty flew close to the window then came back to the level of the boy.

"Open the window. I am going to look for your book." said Marty to Gavin.

Gavin opened the window and Marty went out leaving the children to prepare themselves to go to bed. He looked for the book where he had fought with Rory but he did not find it. He walked close to the fence and found the book on the grass. He took the book in his claws and suddenly had a vision of danger.

Marty dropped the book; he closed his eyes and concentrated. He watched Marvel and a troop of birds searching for them. He transformed himself into an Eagle then into a Black Vulture.

He released a black smoke which spread in the night and covered the castle. Marty started reading Marvel's thoughts. She was moving towards Graceland. She was looking for Marty. By her side, was Prior the Bald Eagle, Marty sat on a tree.

He transformed himself into a Jamaican Woodpecker and started to strike the trunk. He sent a message to his comrades in Graceland.

"Toc...Toc...Toc.. Desert the nests. Toc...Toc...Toc.. Marvel's coming with a large army. Toc...Toc...Toc.. Regroup in the caves."

As soon as Marty finished, he returned to the room.

Marty found the children asleep. He changed himself into an old woman and covered them with a duvet. Carla sat down on a chair close to the window.

"Need to prepare a plan because the days to come will be difficult but exciting!" stated the old woman silently.